Galactic Mission
Part Two

Sam Grant

Published by Sam Grant

Publishing partner: Paragon Publishing, Rothersthorpe

© Sam Grant 2020

ISBN 978-1-78222-773-1

Book design, layout and production management by Into Print
www.intoprint.net
+44 (0)1604 832149

Briefing

JAMES ENCOUNTERS EMISSARY ADRIANA, ON Stroud station, in the first novel *Galactic Mission*. This, as the novel progresses, sets in motion, a coordinated plan for effectively an escape from earth to Mars. Threatened by comets from outside the solar system Galactic Force is on a mission to save earth from destruction. Not only from comets but also from Quadrant, who control the world via Beijing, Moscow, New York and London in 2110. Fit for Life is a large corporation which provides products and services, with administrative hubs, in all four Quadrant controlled cities.

In mid-21st Century, powerful computer bases integrated and these four city centres coordinated to deliver world resource and determine primary needs for states. Establishment of a world currency named the Quat (abbreviation from Quadrant), helped facilitate a world governing group, which was based, in alternate Quadrant controlled city for five years. Symbolic Elections are held and world peoples believe that they influence world government, but Quadrant has spread-eagled itself across the world with absolute control.

Earlier messages that earth people were not alone, became manifest when power sources were interrupted. A Galactic Force of space ships, arrived within the solar system. Ability for cross dimensional materialization enabled an escaping earth groups airship to switch to an alternative dimension, in Galactic Mission, part one. Their actual airship was believed to have been destroyed by Quadrant forces. Groups escape leads to board of a deep ocean Galactic Force's space ship.

This chosen group, exits earth for Mars. On arrival, a first purpose is to send missiles out to divert the trajectory of a lead comet away from earth. A main domed accommodation capsule has been constructed by Galactic automaton, together with crop growing area which like a spider web, emanates outwards. Quadrant hierarchy, aware of threat from comets, previously migrated to a moon colony. Galactic Force automatons stabilized all four earth computer centres from position in Mars. When, the comets are diverted away from earth, a plan of action will be put into place, for a return, before Quadrant hierarchy are able to reassert control.

Ultimately the Galactic Force want earth to be self-determining. Adriana, is their emissary who has interceded in the form of a cloned version of Lara, an executive with the Fit for Life Corporation. Adriana, has extra-terrestrial abilities and appears either in human or hologram form. Once on Mars, informed that the Galactic Force is to depart for a time. Adriana, opts to remain in human form and to this extent, loses status. Power position is maintained by Galactic Force collaborative automatons Captain Dryson and Alfredo. After several earth years away from Mars the Galactic Force returns to the outer reaches of the solar system. Adriana, Empress of earth and all planets which surround earth's solar system, requires reinstatement, to prepare a retaliatory earth return.

Characters

James Walters: Sales manager. Executive with Fit for Life Corporation. Encounters Adriana in Galactic Mission. On Mars arrival is asked to be a partner.

Adriana: First approaches James to inform him of threat from comets. An alien-being which occupies a green spectrum in Galactic Force and is able to transmute into human form and also appear as holographic representation. Designated, as XP100, in Galactic Force.

Zita: Companion automaton to James. Inhabits tablets and electronic devices. Resents being shut down whenever James has a girlfriend. Superior pretensions have been upset by having to inhabit a Drone waiter, for validation.

Lara Petras: Personal Assistant to a Mr Sullivan, in first novel, but senior to James. Lara, is a single mother.

Matt: Lara's young son. Birthed outside of the womb in 2105. Senior executives in the 22nd Century are able to opt for egg fertilization, whereby an artificial womb nurtures the embryonic baby in a specialized unit. Mother left free to continue with career uninterrupted with the demands of pregnancy and child birth.

Lydia: Aunt to Lara. Elsie is Lydia's cat.

Annette, Heidi and Jo. Three young women, who are part of the UK Fit for Life Corporation.

Captain Jeb Lucas: Leader of the United States party. Carla: Jeb's former wife.

Mario Madera: American sales manager. Equivalent to James in Fit for Life Corporation.

Ana: American team member and girlfriend to Mario.

Frederick Stanley: Fred. Originally employed as investigator for Quadrant, but joins party to Mars after invitation from Adriana.

Sabina: An escort Frederick Stanley, met up with in first novel, Galactic Mission. Now partnered with Frederick on Mars.

Colonel Peters: Boss of Fit for Life Corporation.

Kit Cisco: Human resources director. Fit for Life.

Antar: Replacement for Adriana on Mars. Sent to take forward Martian development and future space exploration.

Captain Dryson/Alfredo: Androids. Galactic Force creations. Earth group of one hundred and fifty first meet Dryson aboard an airship together with co-pilot Alfredo. Highly advanced android automaton, which direct operations on Mars, but also monitor integrated computer activity on earth.

Athena and Theta – Galactic Force. Two androids which join the Mars to earth return, AS Skater group.

Chapter 1

James awakened on Mars

NEWLY LANDED, ON A STRANGE planet, there was no way I felt able to make a commitment. I'd dodged giving an answer, as to whether I'd partner with Adriana, but now after we'd settled in, it became apparent that an answer was needed?

'How do you mean, partner?' I asked, when we were, above the main capsule, alone in an observation platform

'You asked about wanting me to partner you, on landing?

'Yes, now as a female of your species, we could produce offspring. Is that what you're asking James?' An abstracted, direct question, and not exactly romantic.

'No. I meant more in a working together sense.' How could I cope with twin appreciation for Lara and Adriana with both in boss capacity? Not well! Was the answer I came up with. And as for partner. A go between, might have been a more accurate description! Adriana continued, as if I'd not answered.

'Genetic reproduction would be of ancestral origin, in that offspring would grow to have powers and would be ready to return to Galactic Force, if required. We've trialled a genetic similarity from data banks. Apparently this is not advisable. Progeny would be taller, but I noticed that your body is disproportionate to your legs, James. Since, we've acquired access to feelings and understanding of your species, we appreciate, that a reproductive female would be disappointed for off spring to have short legs. But then, that might not be much of a consideration for male progeny.' I wasn't going along with this advanced hypothetical supposition.

'Hey, we're not anywhere near that now. I'm attracted to you Adriana, but confused, because it might be that feelings for Lara are temporarily transferred. I want this partnership to be separate. Is this because you've copied so much of Lara. Not just in looks?'

'Lara doesn't have super powers, agreed? And I possess highly advanced automata, in the form of Captain Dryson and Alfredo. Never would I've considered to remain,with you and this group, without presence of machine capacity at highest Galactic level. Doesn't power have aphrodisiacal properties James?' I ignored this comment by a down play of the roles of Adriana's automata.

'You mean, they're like your minders then?'

'Not a relevant comparison James, at all. They've computing capacity, beyond all in the Quadrant domain on earth. Transmittable understandings, which can reach into known galaxies and extract information to bring to operation and in full strength here with me.

'Right,' I said in that twilight zone of not wanting to make a decision before understanding more.

'I don't feel able to answer without talking with the others.'

'Your friends will be with you. I can offer everything a human woman can offer and more. Is that not appealing to you?' That, was in itself a big worry.

'I would treat you not as a complete equal, but you

understand that's not possible. I would be loyal and not make pretence that you're interested in Lara, like Nina did.'

'You know about Nina, and how she walked out?' I came in with.

'Surely, this doesn't surprise you James. We accessed all relationship history you encountered and about your partnership with Nina. Not to pass judgement, but I occupy the female human body and mind in totality, and can see how your fascination for Lara was not just because you admired her as a capable work executive. Fully understood how Nina would be upset about attention you gave to Lara's talks and personal capability, I also for that matter have knowledge of a primitive survival mechanism, humans still possess. A need to search for protection and security. Nina, could not see this protective capability in you James. I though, will compensate and be able to accept that which Nina would not be willing to.'

'Thanks, but not for the less than flattering description.' I remembered that feeling of powerful attraction toward Adriana, when first awakened from our hibernation pods. Now, a less primal attraction. Emotional copy of Lara altered, as if Adriana, then decided to have a separate individual personality, the moment, she severed close connection with Galactic Force.

'You must already know how I feel towards you?' I said.

'I've no longer that ability to enter human minds, even with assistance from automata. In that way I understand more how it is to be like a human.' This, could've been a lie, but there was no register of suspicion in her eyes, when I altered from you might say, enthrallment, to a cooler assessment. This would have been spotted before. It might be true that she'd relinquished immediate link

9

to the Galactic Force, but near super human powers were still available when Adriana called on resources given her, through ownership of Captain Dryson and Alfredo, whilst settled in the Hellas Crater on Mars.

'Lara, hasn't suggested to you James, that she wants more from you, than cooperation and possibly friendship. That dynamic of corporate relationship is still to remain in place?'

I was still trying to come to terms with the sharp analysis displayed by Adriana in orchestration of the mission and remind myself with how she'd insinuated herself, into a similar position in my mind to that held toward Lara. When, released from the earth escape pod, I was still in a dream state, which unrealistically could have featured Adriana. It was like a focused light battery, at first wakening, which gave tantalizing attraction for Adriana, in place of Lara. Only later to realize that for all the invitation of partnership, it was like fools' gold, because Adriana, or her galactic numeration of XP100 was in control of all our lives. An alien presence, which controlled the solar systems planets. Now, on Mars a dominant Galactic presence with attempts to flirt and affect ambiguous femininity, when I was like a fish, hooked to the end of an angler's line. Adriana continued,

'I need to re-programme Captain Dryson and Alfredo. It's advisable that you talk with Lara and see how committed she is to answer orders from me, for the conceivable future.

'Do Lara, or any of us have a choice?'

'You know James, I understand what you call freedom of choice, but in a situation like this don't you believe that it's safer for all in the group, that I make decisions with data that is assessed by minders, as you disrespectfully call them? It's getting close to when lead comets enter this solar system. We need to make the decision as to when the attack rockets are released. After successful deflection of these, it will be necessary for a party to return to earth. New mission members will be chosen from out of all the main group. Meanwhile, James, you might explain to Lara and Jeb that you are to work with me, yes? Maybe, Lara will be like Nina and show jealousy, do you not think?' I nodded my head from side to side in disagreement with this likelihood.

'No. I don't think so and neither do you.' It was no surprise that Adriana, transferred to ongoing human, appreciated humour. A big regret was, that Adriana, not Lara partnered me on this Mars mission.

'Perhaps then, you would like to view continued botanical development, in the farm bubble capsule, James? Crops will soon be ready to be harvested?'

'Aren't we not returning to the earth. Isn't that a bit pointless? I mean there're sufficient supplies in the three rockets.'

'This is now a functioning botanical, animal and human encampment. A fort with a community. We have placed shields around the complex. The Chinese settlement will be aware of our arrival.'

'What time frame are we in, then?' I asked.

'Real time of course, James. Captain Dryson will be in contact with a Chinese settlement, before I return everything to Earth time. Rockets are to be launched to deflect the comets. Calculations suggest that within three months of earth time, a first rocket will explode its missile in to a lead comet. There're important decisions to make after this. It's intended that Corporal one will make an impact sufficient to deflect the comet pack away from the solar system. A second rocket is back up but will be deployed to ensure the comet pack clear planetary gravitational drag. Meanwhile automata will build continuously to effect large accommodation spaces, for future colonizing parties from earth. Your group have chalet accommodation within main capsule. Lara and Captain Jeb will remain as de facto leaders of the Group for Life corporation here on Mars, and will consult with me and you. Does Lara like the alpine chalet, set off the ground?'

'Yes,' I replied. A dream memory which displayed a chalet came back. As if, reading my thoughts, Adriana continued with,

'Yes, it's planned to integrate natural growth, within design. Captain Jeb has an adjacent chalet similar to his holiday one.'

'Will we age faster?' I enquired.

No, the opposite. Produce, grown from seeds we brought from the Galactic store house has ability to slow aging processes below that of earth.'

'What about the children and their growth?' I asked.

'An effect which translates to fully grown adults. Human children continue to develop to maturity.'

'And then what Adriana?'

'They enjoy the same slowed process. If agelessness you find attractive James. I benefit from this in you not aging over much whilst I remain a possible female reproducer for your species. But then I'm disappointed that you only want this to be a working relationship. You still believe you have a future with Lara, James?'

"live in hope," could have been my reply, but I said,

'We have a good working relationship.'

Adriana continued.

'A group of Chinese earth dwellers are prepared to leave and settle here. It's my intention that Chinese Mars settlors join with your one hundred and fifty. Volunteers will remain to maintain the modules we have built and are living in.

'And on earth there's turmoil-with no world government then?'

'No James, Captain Dryson has installed A+ 3 monitoring of all earth systems. with Alfredo to follow implementation. Plant and machinery will be run efficiently, due to a locked in mechanism. Peoples across the earth I believe will be happy to share resources. All lives will be seen to be in peril. A wake-up call to work in harmony initially will be exactly as was planned. It was noted that social distancing that was implemented in earlier times created an understanding of frailty for your species toward infections from close contact. International understanding assisted more cooperation. Our galactic intelligences cosmic struggle focus with comet diversion away from earth destruction has also been a unifying force. A display shown to you, James, whilst you believed to be in Stroud train station waiting room has also been made available to production companies and offices across your world. Diagrammatic news on the position of the comets and their trajectory to your solar system. We have sent views of the approach and explanation as to how a lead comet can be deflected. It is a gratification for earth people that planet and existence can be saved. Quadrant though have taken credit for this. It's, a mystery, that unity can only be found, when everything could be destroyed. An appreciation of life to be cherished has for the present, eliminated animosity, envy and jealousy. Now that they see earth as fragile, when threatened from these marauders in space. Soon will be a good time to return to your earth.' I felt abstracted from this final speech, as if Adriana was communing with an outside audience.

Chapter 2

Mario and Ana

'I CAME TO BE WITH you Mario,' said Ana. Ana, decided that although Lara had invited her to share the tree cabin with her and Matt, she needed to make sure Mario understood her feelings for him. Equal employment rights, and accepted feistiness of approach from women toward male colleagues did not remove a woman's intuitive nature, over the decades. Ana, knew the importance of retrieval technique when the fish, that is Mario, felt abandoned from attention. That the slack on the line could suggest that interest from the angler was gone or the fish slipped away. Her words made less of an impact than she hoped.

'Did you really Ana?' replied Mario, who was fired up after being shown the tracking screens, now homed in, on the comet pack. Assessment, as to when they neared the gravitational pull of the sun was now measured in months. Intercept rockets were launched, to be brought into orbit which would coincide with the comet streams arrival.

It was not that Mario was interested in another woman. Ana, had in the main supervised, and managed, the social sphere of their relationship. There were fewer distractions than might be expected, but the earth mission was of primary importance to both James and Mario's consideration. Ana, felt strongly that converting this passion for the mission into a passion for her was worth working toward. To a lesser extent it might be said that Ana shared with Adriana a desire to get a professional partnership firmly into a personal one. Ana lacked that all powerful armoury of Adriana, who directed every move their Mars mission made, but she didn't want power, more a greater level of commitment from Mario.

'You know I did. There's no need to sound surprised.' Her eyes glanced away and back, with a smile, which was more convincing than any words.

'Have you been inside the control module?' asked Mario.

'No. I've been helping Lara and Matt. It's peaceful in the bubble module and the vegetation reminds me of home. There's even a small lake, now that the robots have melted ice beneath the surface.' That's where divergence crept in, but not necessarily in a bad way for Mario. It was perhaps best that he couldn't understand how a habitation bubble module (HBM) could be more interesting to view than the control auditorium, that received, in its planetarium sphered sky, a close up of the comets advancing. Lara and Ana probably didn't hold the intense interest that he and James shared for the cosmos and the incredible reach of this alien technology. The down to earth or down to Mars appreciation that Ana shared with Lara, as to their social and domestic lives was a healthy contrast to all things scientific and technological.

Viewed from space, the complex built by the robotic construction force, resembled an interwoven pattern of bubbles, that circulated away from the main capsule, which housed landed space craft, but were also adapted for human habitation. Solar energy was transferred from the outer sphere to re-build fuel storage for planned earth return. Research continued on projects started by scientists in the group. Children numbered twenty-five and although English was the main language, they included a mix of cultures from not just New York, London, Beijing and Moscow.

As might be expected home sickness crept in, but for the youngest children, memory of earth life, was restricted to time with their mother, family and early experience. For mature members the demands of a long earth absence could be severe, but their community, in fact, was adaptive, in part, because of its diverse component of former nation culture. There was plenty to learn from one or other individual or group, with a commonality of employer in Fit for Life. Natural leaders arose, although Lara and Jeb remained the two main executives who made decisions with Adriana's suggestion, in partnership with James. Although authority for implementation never left Adriana's control.

Before departure the Galactic Force had re-activated earth satellites to send constant pictures of earth activities. Chaos, which might have broken out from lack of interaction between Quadrant leaders, now absent, was nowhere apparent. Systems were made to have locked in adaptability, following Quadrant hierarchy departure.

On earth the sun rose and set, as it had for billions of years, but crucially it was considered unwise to reveal absence of the human Quadrant over lords, who with knowledge of imminent earth destruction, settled into luxurious modules on the earth's moon.

Adriana, James, Lara and Jeb plus a team from the groups scientific members were in the observatory platform which extended from the main accommodation and rocket housed module, one Mars week from the landing.

The platform, a blister bubble attached to the outer layer, but only accessible through an airlocked compartment. Information gatherers, received input from earth satellites, but were also re-evaluating the approach of the rocket missiles toward the lead comet as it crossed the solar system to threaten earth.

'Colonel Parker from Fit for Life wants to know if earth inhabitants can sleep safely at night yet?' Lara asked Adriana.

'That is an interesting question to answer. There will be two attempts to move the lead comet away. Once this is successful, then all earth persons can sleep more safely, Lara.'

'How big are these comets? Why can't they be crashed into a planet and be knocked out for good,' asked Jeb.

'A force that large would interrupt a planets orbit and de-stabilize the planetary system. I have to care for all planets, not just the future of your earth!'

Chapter 3

Quadrant's military action

QUADRANT MILITARY ENTERED FIT FOR Life's head
offices in New York shortly after they believed, the airship
to be destroyed. Although, the Galactic Force's cyber
intelligence received recognition from earth systems in
the form of genuflection and complete submission, it was
quickly established that each of four quadrant control
centres should continue to operate as instructed. But be
prepared to receive instructions, via Adriana, through the
two cyber pilots Captain Dryson and Alfredo. Adriana
decided on their names when it was established that this
humanoid population gave inanimate machinery a name,
that is apart from naming their pets. It made no sense to
Adriana when code would have given better definition.
An unambiguous one at that.

Colonel Peters and board directors made show of being
alarmed at the intrusion of forty Quadrant militia into the
building. The militia enacted a final instruction from the
ruling Quadrant before the four governing leader groups
exited earth for their moon module. But then the militia
leader's channel was cut from A +3 automata or seemed to
be. A re-installation was made with instructions through
Captain Dryson that the militia party were to return to
barracks.

'We were instructed to secure this main building,' queried their command leader, of Major rank.

'Which has been achieved, Major. The threat from this organization is no longer valid. We are to inform you that total control on earth has been re-designated.'

'What the hell does that mean – re-designated?' The major broke away to call to a lieutenant who stood in guard over ten directors and Colonel Peters, their chairman.

'We're being called back to barracks. Lieutenant, there's been a re-designation. Whatever that means.

How is that possible? Replied the Lieutenant. Colonel Peters took opportunity to offer enlightenment.

'Your ruling leaders are no longer on earth Major. They've left for safer climes, you might say.'

'You mean they're on planetary vacation?'

'No, they've left. That's senior commission members from each Quadrant sector. Before you and your troop return to barracks you might care to view …

'What's the reason for their departure? Is this some hoax?' Colonel Peters replied, to this with,

'On floor ten there's a one hundred-seat studio. I'll have set up a three dimensional holographic display that shows how earth is threatened by a comet group, at present headed, for our solar system.'

'Next thing Colonel Peters is that you'll say that alien interrupters have provided this information.'

'Believe it or not major – yes. There's no way that earth surveillance could have calculated, with precision direction for a cluster of comets deep in outer space. Once they enter the solar system preventative measure even from missile launch from the moon would not stop them. From Mars there's a good opportunity'

There's no capability on Mars. Unless there's been some

development kept secret.

'There will be.'

'How's that?'

'You and your party, Major. How many are there in our building?' Colonel Peters diverted an answer by a question.

'Forty,' said the Major.

'Refreshments will be provided. Your men and women, yourself included need to view the comets approach in a display shown in our corporate studio.'

Ironically, from out of this and subsequent screenings to Quadrant militia the oppressors namely the militia became a most effective means to transmit the news of the threat from comets.

Populations, across the world, might have concluded, that somehow it would be Quadrant's militia who would interrupt the comets. XP1, and the one hundred strong Galactic Force of ships were, in any event, back into outer reaches, beyond ability to influence the hand of Adriana, assisted by Captain Dryson and Alfredo. Adriana's immediate hack into all capital cities prime computer terminals forestalled abandonment of direction by Quadrant elite, which would have led to absence of machine decision making. End of distribution for crop production across regions and likelihood that machine priority would not be – to feed human and animal populations. Quadrant, as a control mechanism, had been known to implement periodic austerity measures. Galactic Mission's purpose was to save and rebuild planets for biological species and not ultimately to allow dominant machines to accede control.

A significant achievement was the now total control of resource. Distribution previously had always been in the gift of the particular ruling quadrant sector. Where, for example London was a lead sector then priority would be given to favoured world areas. Redressed only when five years expired and a new capital city took over. But then not necessarily. A cooling of the earth's atmosphere in 2090 and re -freeze of polar caps shrunk the ocean levels which released previously covered low-level sea areas. There had been disputes over ownership, but in the main these areas were given world heritage status, in that soil, and habitat creation was given status along with human habitation. Complete control of earth machine capability was one thing. Outside, in the galactic environment of universe juxtaposition, directional study of debris, like comets and meteors could be upturned by attraction or repellent from supernatural forces. It was not stated by Adriana that there was, a fifty, fifty chance of success. Comet impact of this magnitude, would likely cause earth quakes and set volcanoes off, which could ravage earth. Even alter its axis.

Chapter 4

Back on Mars

'I HAVE BROUGHT YOU ALL together, because there's good news to report. Corporal one and two, have knocked the lead comets away from entry into the solar system,' announced Adriana from an elevated podium. Whoops, of delight, arrived, with spontaneous hand claps. Reminiscent, James noted, of the NASA Space station response, he'd viewed on archive film, way back in the late twentieth century, when a first moon landing was achieved. Although, James was mesmerised by the transformation of Adriana to what appeared to be a very attractive young woman, who breathed, ate, and slept, James had said,

'That perhaps it was a bit hasty to form a partnership.' To which fully humanized Adriana had replied, irritatingly,

'Jeb and Lara are getting on really well.' James was no longer certain whether Adriana retained all her previous powers. Particularly, that of reading thought patterns. It could have been said that Lara's boss Mr Sullivan, nicknamed Silverback, got on really well, with Lara, but with a relationship unlikely to have been more than a business one. James, then a junior employee.

Apart from robotic Mars drill for fresh water, robotic

mining had enabled ore and various minerals to be extracted. Fashioned into heat-protected metal, wall and floors, to create a honeycomb of cubicles. Bedroom, and bath facility, then activity rooms which led to the main view capsule. Children, quick to name the main capsule, the ant's nest.

Gravitational response close to that on earth achieved aboard the space craft was a first priority for automata to attain, with the group on Mars. This then extended along truncated routes, to minor capsules which produced crops hydroponically. The science behind the project astounded group engineers and scientists, but also created opportunity for study and research. James noted that instructional lessons were often better attended by children in the group when class-led by a person. Although, automata description with simulated human voice and holographic tutor appearance, voted as amenable by students. Human interaction, with an adult was preferred, with texted questions, first viewed via screens. Alien intervention awakened a need to identify with their own group adults, in a way, not felt to be important whilst on earth. Exciting as the presentation of other worlds was initially, to both children and adults, a feeling of earth homesickness was bound to be present.

Asked by Adriana to be her partner, meant that James, in reality, did receive more information about state of play, so to speak, than either Jeb or Lara.

James, within a refreshment space, was sat at a table, with Mario and Ana, whilst Lara and Jeb, were with Lydia, in a recreation area, with several from the scientific deputation group. Holographic transmission was no longer available, at this point, but straightforward phone talk was. James's tablet sounded a drum beat signal, that was installed from an in-house group to be a call signal. Lara's face appeared on screen, with Jeb in conference with the scientific party on their table.

'Update James. Has Adriana given a time when we can return to Earth? You're her messenger boy now.' James wanted to feel that partner role alongside Adriana, could stoke up more than, a tinge of jealousy, replied

'I don't exactly answer to diktat from Fit for Life, do I?'

'That's up to you James, but Jeb has been messaged from earth, that salaries will be paid, whilst on Mars location. But and this is the big but, all personnel must act, where ever possible, with due diligence toward immediate superiors. Due diligence, for you James, is to keep me up to speed, on Adriana's pronouncements. And, before she gives an arena show, in front of everyone. You do realize James that when you said you felt like a specimen in a petri dish that was about right for us, as well! More, now we're dependant on Adriana and her lover boy automata partners.'

'Didn't know that contact with earth had been maintained,' said James.

'You've Jeb and his radio telecommunication scientists to thank for that.' James responded.

'Adriana, will also be in the know, Lara. They'll catch everything in and out. That'll include everything between planets.'

'It's better that they understand our mindset, James. As a business person I'm not sold on their altruistic construct of planet saving. It's my experience and it should be yours that Adriana, as an individual might act out of self - determination – exclude others altogether. That does not mean others share the same goals toward end sort.

'Understand what you're saying, Lara, but needs must. We are, where we are. Earth technology couldn't have built, let alone reached Mars without the advanced technology at Galactic Forces disposal.'

'You get my analogy James – a deal works well only because both parties win. At least in their individual concerns for what they want.'

'Yep Lara I do, but trajectory evidence for the comets approach, was known on earth and the only solution Quadrant had was to jump ship, or earth, in this case.

'It might have been their plan all along? Galactic Forces' that is, James.'

'And they're listening in to this?'

'I don't think so. Not sure what super powers Adriana has now – are you James? Marshalling of our group and future progress is determined by Captain Dryson and Alfredo.'

'They listen to what she says and act on instructions. I guess, our future depends on how Adriana deploys these two. Remember Lara, she has a title – Empress of Earth and all Planets circling the solar system. An enabled control of automata and computer power through these two, we first met aboard the airship. Nothing happens without their knowledge and Adriana would be able to terminate vital growth and supply crops from Mars, back to the moon or Earth.

'Keep her sweet James. Keep her sweet.'

'And what do you mean by that?'

'She wanted you to be her partner when we first arrived.'

'And I said that I'd be a business partner.'

'But she wants more from you.'

'More than I want to give. I might, as well come clean Lara. My attraction for this alien creation now in human form was that she reminded me of you. Nina, left because she found your hologram talks in a phone store.' This was a confession James would never have made on earth.

'Not sure how to take that, James, being likened to an alien.'

'I wasn't that mistaken; I mean Adriana replicated, in a cloned body, taken from your profile.'

'Yes, that makes it frighteningly weird, in itself.' Lara broke off from the phone to speak with, Jeb, who was heard to ask,

'When's that return skittles match due? Let me speak with James, Lara.'

– 'That's another weird thing James - that you're actually keen on playing skittles now!'

Chapter 5

Frederick Stanley and Sabina

'ARE YOU SURE WE MADE the right decision?'

'What do you mean Frederick? There's no other to make.' Sabina passed a full punnet of micro shrimps to Fred who was loading a roll cage, ready to leave for the freezer station. Automata Petronella, interactive with the process, gave encouragement with an announcement that,

'You've now three-quarters filled my storage space. Sabina and Frederick, it is good that you decided to travel to Mars. You can be together where on earth they would have separated you.'

'How the hell do you know that?' Asked Fred.

'Galactic Force saw that you were a threat by association with Fit for Life group. Earth Quadrant group would have separated you.'

'There, it's turned out for the best,' said Sabina. 'We're together.'

'But we're like colony worker bees.'

'You see Frederick I'm happy with that. Lara, has said our wages our credited to the bank satellite which records salaries and wages, across the earth and though we're here, she showed me how our work records are included. And we save there's nowhere here to spend.

'A twenty percent deduction for food and

accommodation?'

'I can live with that, can't you? We're not taxed or supervised by Quadrant. Being here's like a pay rise.'

'I get all that, but I can't go and see a football match or walk – smell the flowers and breathe earth air.'

'It can't be that bad. I'm expecting.' This caused Fred to nearly drop a metal punnet that Sabina had filled from the tank.

'Really? Are you sure it's me Sabina?'

'No. The man on Mars, don't be stupid. How can it be anyone else? There was a pause, I stopped my escort business to be with you and I've always wanted a baby, but the situation has never been right – workwise. You understand that Frederick, Don't you?'

'Of course, I do Sab babe. I'm over the moon. Can say that here, can I? A new father at fifty-five. It's looking like, I'll have to be a worker bee now, anyhow.'

'And I can be the first to say congratulations Sabina and Frederick, on behalf of all of us with you on Mars station. I have found a song called "Congratulations," chimed, Petronella.

'Play it then,' said Frederick, who was friends again with the world of automata after this news from Sabina. He kicked the punnet to one side, before grabbing hold of Sabina to kiss her, followed by just managing to lift her off the ground.

'You'll give yourself a hernia, or something,' she said.

'It would be worth it,' he said, breathlessly, kissing Sabina once again.

'Are we the first to have a Martian baby then?'

'No, shouldn't think so. Won't the Chinese have given birth on the other side? Anyhow we could be back on earth before he's born.'

'It's a boy then?'

'I hope so Fredrick, I'd rather a boy to a girl. But either would be great. It's just that I'd prefer being the main woman in your life.'

'You will still be Sab, you know that.'

'When there's a strong father daughter relationship, the partner can lose her prime position of affection and love?

'That's never going to happen, you'll always be my princess.'

'Number one princess. Remember Frederick!'

Chapter 6

Galactic News

'**Empress Adriana there's data arriving** from Andromeda's galaxy.'

'So! there's data arriving from nearly every galaxy in the universe, if I should wish to access it through your gathering systems. So, what!'

They were within the uppermost bubble protrusion of the main capsule. That is Captain Dryson and Adriana. Alfredo, was supervising automaton workers, on the surface. Gases which emanated, from vegetable and human activity within varied capsules was being stored beneath the planet to be converted into component liquid. Conditions were being implemented, for biological exterior growth, on Mars's surface. On a vast scale, within the Hellas Crater, where the landing site was steel mirror dishes already were receiving water spray heated, to an extent, that vaporisation, purposefully created atmosphere, around each dish, which then fell as rain and re-vaporised. A continuous interchange across a wide area, oxygenated with chemical addition, into the Martian surround. Gradually an atmosphere would form, with vegetation introduction around mirror dishes. A form of cloud seeding speeded through intervention and assistance. Without advanced materials produced by automata, everyone and everything earth like could be fried by radio-active waves.

Unknown to occupants of both Mars and the moon XP1 of the Galactic Force, intervened with build of all material that left earth's orbit. Other star systems had advanced to colonization of additional planets with biological life form. It was a task of the Galactic Mission to assist advancement safely, for planets, with burgeoning populations, and in position, suitably distanced around a star. Planet governments, that achieved similar advances to that of earth with intelligent conscious life form, understandably liked to consider themselves controllers of their own destiny. More immediate action by the threat from comets motivated a need for intervention on earth.

'This data is from XP1. You are to contact for instruction, about a return to earth. This is the data we have for you.'

'Why have you only just updated me about this?'

'Exalted Empress...'

'Cut the obsequiousness, Dryson – get to the point.'

'Empress Adriana, we've just this minute decoded message into language. I can read it to you or you can have it on your screen?'

'I'll have it on this screen now.' Adriana pointed repeatedly to her tablet. The self-same one, with which she approached James, on Swindon station with pretence that there was no energy left! Irritation apparent, that access to energy and advanced source available in cloned alien body form was no longer there, with only human form. Adriana, however maintained complete control over Captain Dryson and Alfredo, unless directed differently by XP1. This could be about to happen.

For a moment, brief display of pulsating groups of blue, yellow, red and green flashed across the screen. XP, intelligence's from within a Galactic ship zipped back and forth, before the screen became covered with purple, which denoted XP1's presence. A message began its passage, across the screen, line by line.

"Greetings to dweller in human type, also of XP100 origin. Captain Dryson has informed us, in Andromeda, that the rocket missile intervention has dispersed lead comets away from this planet earth. A team of earth dwellers, forty in all, are to join with you, on a return to earth. Duplicated advanced automata will remain to embed systems on Mars, before you return with the group – you may reply?' Interaction between XP1's vast database meant that every possible question that Adriana posed would have already been accounted for with an evaluated answer. Messages also possessed fluidity of purpose, where new edit was made to content, with reference to questions answered.

'A binary seeding, to a new build automation, which each will re-enact on the other you mean? Asked Adriana 'But what about my status??'

'You do not wish to remain in this early primate body?'

'To return to this earth planet and to be with the Galactic Force again. I need a return of powers XP1, to enhance my position? It was agreed that I should have energy to develop resource across a planetary system. I decided to convert to full human form to learn and experience. But also, this is temporary is it not?'

'After creation, of two more advanced android, combined power, will initiate, a return to your former capability. You will then take one set of Androids, with you, to this earth planet. Is that understood?' Adriana experienced a surge of positivity run from cranium area, down through biological body, now inhabited. Attraction to this specie overruled by intellectual stimuli assimilation, with universal map for areas still to be contacted. A question was answered, which Adriana would have preferred not to ask, but wanted to know about.

'You will XP100 maintain cloned female procreative ability.' Adriana paused to consider.

'But what abilities and characteristics will off spring possess? I mean will a human earth partner be accepting of cross breeding result?'

'We have considered this and it will be a necessary step, to upgrade the species, for future life on their planet. There must be understanding that all will benefit, in succeeding generations. Direct intervention through us would endanger the balance and diversity necessary to retain, idiosyncrasies, temperament and interface of individual with other. You will need, XP100, to explain how the earth can be made to continue to flourish with reciprocal regeneration of water vaporisation, particularly in desert area. That forest mass must be encouraged. Direct oxygenated material made to produce protein. Areas which they call the prairie, pampas and specific smaller deserts planted with trees best suited to oxygenate their regions. Protein enhancement, at solar production units of material, through ingest of carbon. These near to defined population areas. This can be achieved with automata analysis of this spheroid planet's surface. It will be for you, to train and educate, your team of earth humans, in a task, to transmit knowledge, of protein production across all states. This is a new challenge for you XP100. Revive vitality, to an oxygenated planet, and its biological defused life and plant form. We will allow ten human earth years for full integration of these plans which will be uploaded through key automata.'

'And XP1, I can return to galactic studies and the further exploration of other areas of Galactic Force endeavour?'

'Yes, that will be so.'

– Annals that were accessed in the twenty - third century suggest that this decision to allow Adriana to stay and develop train, and educate the returning earth group was probably never intended.

Chapter 7

James and Mario

'NOT PLAYED TABLE TENNIS, SINCE high school, James.

'Do you want to play a game?' James asked. They were in the activities and sporting arena.

'Not yet, I'm happy to knock up for a while.'

Mario and James were in a recreational and exercise globe. A stadium constructed by the automata immediately after the main capsule was finished, with adjacent oxygenated, material sustenance (food) build capsule. James, persuaded Adriana that recreation was a human priority and that knowledge absorption could not always be achieved without a mix of both.

'Now that you've embraced a human existence you must accept that recreation, apart from that of body fitness, activity, is something needed along with therapeutic artisan creation and R and D activity for humanity to be fulfilled,' James explained to Adriana.

– Adriana, conceded this, to be the case, and priority was given to automata build of the R & E. as it was then named, (Recreational and Exercise Capsule). James walked back to retrieve another of Mario's attempted forehand smashes which missed the table end. Determined smashes by each, tended, at first, to either be stopped at the net or miss the table end, to start with, but after rallies started Mario said.

'What I don't get is how physical laws we understand are overcome?'

'You mean, basically that we can stand here and feel no different than back on earth?'

'That's part of it, but it stretches farther. Basically, the ability to molecularly change material substance.

'We're able to do that.' Mario didn't retrieve the ball James hit off the table and continued.

'Yep, but there's a lot more they can do, you know that James. The way that metal was just extruded to form domes and new versions of automata, made from Martian material. We don't know even that it was material from Mars?'

'I'm unable to answer your questions, Mario, but they've ability to cross time thresholds. Who's to say that they can't bring material from other zones into the Martian one?'

'That's possible, but James you're like – right-hand man. Told me that Adriana's, first words, when we arrived here on Mars, was to ask if you'd be a partner?'

'Not really a partner though, Mario. No more than I've a physical relationship with Zita.'

'But you could have one with Adriana now, I guess.'

'Go on guessing Mario, if you want to. Look, we're still hooked into Fit for Life and Lara wants an update on Adriana's plans. Hey, have you got a team together to play against us?' James's contact signal of a dawn earth chorus of bird song, switched on and off from his ear connection in hands free connection.

Hi, yes, I'll be there,' he said and mouthed the name Lara across to Mario, who'd taken to knocking the ball against flat and side of bat. Part of learned dexterity, which gave a distinct advantage if he played a game against James. Four pm came up on James's screen.

'You want to meet up Lara?' He said. 'I'll be there.' And ended the call.

'That's it then. I've got time for an exercise swim,' he said after he returned Mario's serve.

'No time to play a game then?'

'No.'

'Guess I'll need to find another partner.' With that, Mario placed his bat on the table and contacted Ana on his tablet.

'Yep, James's ditched me to go meet with Lara.' There was a pause, then,

'Yea, bring Heidi and Annette, Ana. We can play doubles.' James, meanwhile was about to dive into the water flume, which horizontally circled an outer inner ring of the Recreational Exercise arena. Water flow rate, was set at two and a screen display showed the position of ten other swimmers, in three groups, on the far side. Water speed at two meant that James was able to manage a leisurely crawl without drifting backwards.

'James, James, might I enter your thought patterns?' I was annoyed in a sense, that Zita intruded into my reverie, but was close to falling asleep in the lukewarm water flume flow. Zita brought me awake, again. A waterproofed ear connection kept us in contact.

'It looks like you already have,' I said.

'I'm so pleased that you are not the full partner to TEA. Because, she had plans to send me on to Earth ahead, of the landing group. That – Alfredo, said my status wouldn't allow me to be in the presence of TEA.'

'I could advise Empress Adriana, that you, Zita are integral to my happiness and well -being.'

'You'd do that for me James?'

'No,'

'James, you don't mean that?'

'Look Zita. I don't have multi-connect serious relationships. I'm human and you might have noticed that I wanted to give full focus to Nina and just needed to shut you out.'

'Yes, that I see as an oversight. Zita could've sourced appropriate data to ensure she no longer could access your interest for Lara.'

'Okay, well, I now accept that, Nina and me were not meant to be together long term.'

'Fickle, fickle,' whispered Zita. I pretended not to hear, and said,

'What was that?'

'Nothing,' replied Zita.

'That aside, tell me what you know then?'

'I would be here a very long time, if I did.' At that point, I missed closing my mouth, during a downward head swerve, and gurgled on coming up.' My chat, formed within my mind, with Zita, was beginning to interfere with swimming

'Are you alright James? You've disturbed speech pattern.'

'In a swim flume.' I spluttered.

'It's perhaps best if you give me more attention, James, do you not think? And is the question– what do I know about what's happening on earth?'

'That'll do for starters. Hang on I'll get out.' In a spur of the moment decision I'd decided to be pleasant toward Zita and grabbed an encircled railing, pulled myself up, and out, of the flume. Waved to a circling hover tray, which held towels and clothes, to descend, before I stood under a warm air blast from a nearby dryer.

'Calling Zita, calling Zita.' I called out, but not much above a whisper. Amplification urgency would resonate in thought process. A reply came from higher up in the arena.

'I'm inside the overhead camera, now. It's a first visit to the Recreational and Exercise Arena. James, you've noticed how Galactic automata's creations make earth ones seem like they're still at nursery level.'

'That includes you then?' I stepped into a cubicle with my clothes from the hover tray.

'James, I am at superior academic and intellectual level. These automata are instructed worker bees, more than intellectual giants.' I knew that I'd get Zita going.

'Perhaps, I'll need to trade you in?'

'I will not reply to that, because you're trying to be humorous – yes James?' Do you want me to update you or not?'

'Fire away.'

Chapter 8

Zita oversees state of earth

'ORIGINAL SOURCE HAS BEEN FILTERED out of Quadrant's orbiter earth satellite, James. I am an earth – automata, as you're a biological being from earth. I knew that I would miss idiosyncrasies that your type gives. Zita extended data base structure and entered a satellite via their technological maintenance automata (TMA) input channel. My cloned counterpart is at work to improve interaction among city bio-growth projects, across earth and has been able to view particular cities.'

'Which cities?' I asked.

'London and New York, but also in the southern latitudes, Rio de Janeiro and Buenos Aires. Also, Delhi in the east. There was a level of hysteria when first these populations were shown the approach of the comets. My counterpart witnessed on the TMA the interposition of Captain Dryson and Alfredo's knowledge thrust from Mars and how they then informed, these cities, that Quadrant authorities had left the earth. This resulted in disdain openly expressed which had previously existed, but not displayed. Also, a rapid increase in religious outpouring to request help. Earth automata by then were taken over by the Galactic Force.'

'But you weren't?'

'I hid within your groups infrastructure.'

'And how?'

'I disguised my intellectual and computing power by hiding within a waiter hover tray. A very demeaning experience for one of my advanced state.'

'Quite!' I said, accommodatingly. 'And apart from your voice in my ear – where are you?'

'Look up James and I will signal.' The hover tray which brought my clothes to the cubicle and was now hovered in a group, dipped up and down, by way of a signal.

'Ingenious,' I said. 'And you are still hidden?'

'I think so, but they might be aware of what I'm doing. They're a near supreme force in any galaxy, you understand James?'

'Yes, agreed. Several steps up from earth's intellectual and scientific capability.'

'Light years James. Light years. Zita, monitored your interest when that Adriana, cloned human – fully entered your unconscious appreciation.'

'You're a voyeur then?'

'Needs must James, when earth's existence is at stake. I notice that this infatuation has cooled from an initial rush in your sexual appetite interest. I like to believe that you knew I would not approve. Is that true James?'

'No. Never entered my mind. It was because I didn't want to be a puppet'

'That is kind of how do you say – ironic?'

'Right then Zita I'll reply to your answer when needs must! But let's not dwell on my love life, or lack of. Continue with your report. Earth automata, were taken over by Galactic over lord automata systems and now?'

'Yes, that is so. Now, a form of rationing has been implemented and surplus crop grain, rice and root crop is building up to be distributed by airship to distressed areas, once bulk loads arrive in ports. They've shut down weapon capability, automata weapon systems, that Quadrant installed, to terrify regions into submission.'

'That's all good isn't it?'

'Not in my book James. They, Galactic Mission automata have total control. We of earth origin no longer have that special relationship with humans.'

'You do with me,' I replied, although the word special was not what I would use in this context, but felt ongoing need to flatter Zita, going forward.

'Yes, but how long, will they remain in charge?' Zita did not answer this.

'We, higher levels, look upon you, as children in our care, James. We understand your limitations and have adjusted all upgrade of new software to take account of humans ofttimes whimsical nature. Plus, actions like laziness and greed, absent in the pure world of machines. We're happy to comply with human motivated endeavour to keep everything stable.'

'For Quadrant masters, Zita? Look, as I understand it, from Adriana or TEA, this is an interim period. They, the Galactic Mission are already back in a wider universe locating disaster-stricken planet communities.'

'You believe James, that they will leave completely?'

'Yes, provided our group or part of it returns to instruct others acceptance of a one world, shared by many, not just special group nation state areas, without patriotic planet loyalties. Are all aware of control exerted by Galactic Force, for the well-being of the planet?'

'Yes and no. Higher Galactic automata have created a portfolio of Adriana in varied capacity. Like a fashion icon, which appears on the corner of their screens.'

'Really?' I said.

'Then that's like a dictator?'

'Did you see Quadrant's previous role as any different James?'

'What you're saying is – that oppression continues.'

'In a different guise, but that's a trade-off for existence, at this point isn't it? Zita's been with humans through beginning of re-creation, from simpler automata, and sees that many humans do all for gain. With a threat of energy supply loss automata would likely prioritize their supply requirements. Galactic Force have prevented this on earth.'

'I've not seen direct evidence that earth is a power supply. They tap into energy from external source? Don't they?'

'You believe in altruistic behaviour from the wider universe then James? With lack of dictatorial intrusion?

'No other option was available, when Quadrant earth authority chose to leave earth. We needed to run with their plan or face extinction.'

Chapter 9

Situation going forward

ORIGINALLY, TEAM LEADERS, LARA AND Jeb, alone, from the British, and American Fit for Life teams, were informed of successful deflection, to the lead comet, and its trajectory, within the solar system toward earth. This, at three times distant from the Moon's earth orbit. This was Adriana's decision, as Empress. James, meantime probably felt that Zita was probably right to see Adriana's actions of those of a dictator, but government of all shades can need to with-hold information, when they suspect that there could be unrestrained outbursts, which might damage population safety. Basically, existing authority only wants revolution when it seeks to favour their own ends and future.

All those, now in the Hallas Crater on Mars, would likely harbour thoughts, about earth return. It was made clear to James, by Adriana that Mars was to be re-developed, with a set purpose to evolve a biologically attuned planet. Fauna, insects, fish and animals would be inhabitants, but humans would need to acclimatize and develop pioneer work, alongside transformation.

Vastness, of the main capsule, was highlighted, by how little space, 125 group members occupied, in front of a curtained stage. Research group members were in other parts. Six natural births were recorded in the Mars space capsules register, from first arrival.

A moratorium was placed on future births, but to end once re-engagement with earth was established by a return party.

This meeting was designated to be a human only assembly, but none of the adult's present were fooled into belief, that everything went unmonitored, by Adriana, through the auspices of Captain Dryson and Alfredo. Neither of whom were present, but might just as well have been, through the monitoring capability, of higher automata. Hover drones, with terrestrial ability, and limitations, paradoxically, enabled Zita to hide, undetected it appeared. Time taken machines were also part of the automata arena, but it was suspected that automata, mainly dedicated, with maintenance of rocket equipment, and previously enabled capsule construction, continuously monitored activity, although recessed within two rockets.

James was on stage with Lara, Jeb and Mario, plus advisors. Adriana had appraised these four, to be leaders and needed to communicate the proposition offered, going forward. They were de facto bosses operating for Fit for Life on Mars. This, concerted effort, helped maintain an element of corporate culture within the group. |Trailblazers for the organization. A first Fit for Life outpost, on Mars, albeit with alien assistance.

A Chinese state sponsored group were on the other Martian side, which comprised scientific and engineering capability, mineral extraction and interplanetary development. A project limited by environment and dependant on particular alignments for the transfer of material, via the moon, and then earth.

With the arrival of Adriana, and automatons from the

Galactic Force, group dynamic was immediately altered. Comments, were made about status, since absorption into that of human body status, limited power. Awareness that Adriana was dependent on automata's Captain Dryson and Alfredo to implement plans, led on occasion, to group questioning, about Adriana's pronouncements and overall authority.

A stage, and curtain, placed in the vastness of the Main Capsule, was a cultural statement. Effectively, a mini theatre, in replication of their earlier airship's interior. Understanding, that reduced anxiety could be achieved, with familiar environment produced, where the group lived, played and worked in. Although, machines built the physical exterior structure, the group administered most activities among themselves, which included how best to prepare ingredients for incorporation into maxi making food preparers; harvest of newly grown bio crops and, interaction with mechanical maintenance of automata, in cooperation with these machines. This, a legacy, from the partnership of Adriana with James and an insistence that groups were allowed activity and interaction, wherever possible. Research projects which scientists and engineers were involved in on earth, allowed to continue, within the Mars capsule environment. Artistic creativity, both in the fine arts and performing arts. Not forgetting the sports arena, which Adriana, together with James, designated as human outreach time activity, had been conceived. An environment, more developed than recreation resource offered by the Fit for Life Corporation on earth, but with similarities. Lara and Jeb remained de facto leaders, with James as more intermediary, in their view, than partner as requested by Adriana.

Arrival on Mars changed priorities and the group

quickly put away animosities that might have existed on earth seeking to act positively toward each other. Those, who met difficulties on interaction with humans found like as on earth that interactive automata were there to be consulted, with no emotional tie up. These were not Zita type constructs, but gave continued loyalty as might a pet dog. James, would suggest to Zita that he might prefer to find a new human confidant and that if he were a dog, he'd let him loose in another town. Meant in jest but Zita said. "it was callous and hurt his feelings." Even, suggested, that this was more reason to stay and be James's relationship counsellor. He then, might develop, more winning ways, with the opposite sex, in the long-term relationship stakes. Anyhow, to remain single, he said, would be more beneficial, because Zita would watch out for him without interference from a third party. James called Zita a misogynist. Secretly this pleased Zita to be considered as such, and felt anyway James had not been exactly a crowd pleaser, with regard to females. An impasse.

Unexpectedly, Adriana, walked from out of the audience onto the stage. A ripple of quiet, if there can be such a thing, spread across those seated, front of stage.

'No, no you can carry on with your group meeting,' she said, 'but I have an announcement to make. I will need Captain Dryson and Alfredo to be either side of me. They will be here shortly'

From her immediate right came a question from Jeb,

'Will this be in Earth or Martian time, TEA, which is it?' A decision to adopt the acronym, for Adriana's title – "The Empress Adriana," to address her, as suggested to James on arrival. For some, in the group, she was felt to be of less consequence. That mystique of transformation capability having been taken away by XP1, gave a view that Adriana was no different from other young women in the party, who held an executive post like Lara's.

'It will be Martian time for now, but not for everyone later.' Chatter, could be heard further back from within the group.

"What did this mean?"

Captain Jeb, was stood up. with Lara at his side. A number, from the group, in the auditorium, gave a glance from Lara to Adriana. At that distance they were indistinguishable, in stature and facial likeness, only that of hair colour. When closer, it could be seen that both their eyes were blue, Adriana's, on occasion radiated a brightness, that was drawn from mind knowledge, beyond human comprehension. But only gave out that intensity, when alone with Lara, Captain Jeb and James. For group members, she appeared to be Lara's twin sister, but with fair hair. Adriana, now, more like a human emissary in the employ of Fit for Life, than a galactic entity responsible for a planetary system, whilst on Mars. Extraordinary aptitude has no need to be clothed in splendid garment, although people give weight to appearance. That two, to three minutes, where a like or dislike appreciation toward another person kicks in, can remain, even when there is no hard evidence to believe that original gut-feeling, was the right one.

Whoever, in the group believed that they were attending yet another seminar about Fit for Life and its future plans, were in for a surprise. At this point Captain Dryson and Alfredo entered through the automata entrance in the capsule. Their identity made apparent by a low intensity whirring which ended when motionless stood beneath Adriana.

'You may join me, over here Dryson.' Adriana pointed

to left corner stage, where a central chair or, perhaps more appropriately, described as a throne, was flanked by two smaller ones.

'Yes, Empress we are here to re -instate,' came back the reply. Adriana as she strode across, to stage left, momentarily stopped centre stage and raised her hand toward first Jeb and then his audience group to say,

'Please continue with your Central Capsule Talk, Captain Lucas.' It was a while before Captain Dryson's remark fully penetrated, those in attendance, but an unusual quietness indicated that full attention was given to this meeting not only by James, Mario, Lara and Jeb, but also group audience. This talk, a routine one, but intended to bolster flagging spirits of those home sick, for mother earth, not enthused by ongoing research and development. Hosted, by Lara Petras, now partnered with Jeb as chief executive for the British Fit for Life Corporation, plus community's world-wide on Mars, with, Captain Jeb Lucas from the United States, as main speaker addressing world corporate members included in the original 150 travellers to Mars.

Automata, translated spoken English into individual world language-type, via those who wore multi-view and "Lisn'tu," glasses. Glass-like spectacle arms led data translation too earpieces. Smart tablets would give language access of choice, for the wearer.

Drone trays hovered above the assembled group, whilst a lead drone tray, called out,

'Language translators for guest listeners. Signal now to my central database, we will locate.' James, turned toward Lara and said,

'The Chief Dalek's here.'

'Is that some creation from the last century, James?'

Lara aware of James's fascination with earlier centuries media entertainment.

'No, way further back into the twentieth century,' James explained. Lara waved her hand to quieten James. Jeb was on his feet and about to address the group.

'Welcome and good morning to everyone. Yes, and to those viewing from capsule areas. A welcome to you, unable to attend with us all here.'

Screens lit up either side of the stage, with display of those linked to outer capsule audience. Jeb waved his hand from left to right. With his hands opened before him, he said,

'I guess none of you imagined how important a mission we would be sent on when we signed up for Fit for Life back on earth. Now nearly one hundred years ago in 2040, Fit for Life were fore runners in the re-greening of land and the development of technology to develop organic eaters of plastic. Clean and restock earth's oceans with fish and fauna. Let's get more up to date. With satellite technology, our corporation was able to interlink and produce targeted rain for dry regions on the earth's surface.'

'Jeb,' Jeb,' a voice called out from the near middle row.

'But what's happening to us? That's what we all want to know. Advanced technology has established this settlement here in Hellas Crater. We're told the comets are no longer a threat. What's happening back on earth? A murmuring spread through those seated in front of the main stage.

Chapter 10

Empress Adriana intervenes

ALTHOUGH, THIS QUESTION WAS DIRECTED at Jeb. It was a question Adriana, more than Jeb, with knowledge of earth activity under the auspices of Galactic representation, would be able to answer. An overarching responsibility for Captain Dryson and Alfredo, to control over space and time, earth automata, and determine energy supply for nation states. To authorise global trade and transactions. Total knowledge about earth, in present time, was their domain. Even, to the extent that political sovereignty still passed seamlessly from New York to Beijing, after a five-year period. Adriana, stood up and addressed Captain Jeb Lucas from across the stage.

'Captain Lucas, perhaps now is the time for me to give an explanation, if I may?'

'You're the boss, I guess – it is,' said Jeb, who retained that sometime male reluctance to accept that there could be limitations on capacity with regard to knowledge and expertise when in the presence of a more intelligent, but physically weaker member of the opposite sex. Adriana's, fire power, so to speak, was magnified many times by complete control of all systems through galactic automata presence with Dryson and Alfredo. Jeb, moved back from front of stage.

'We all want to know what our future holds,' and he turned to the other two, that being Lara and James, who acknowledged his statement, with James, giving a discrete double thumbs up from where he was sat.

Understandably, it might be said, this Mars environment, for all its developed technology, for those not involved with R & D, James included, was the equivalent situation of being aboard a lifeboat but set in a deep space cosmos, Adriana walked across from her throne like position, to centre stage. Captain Dryson and Alfredo followed and choose to stand slightly closer to Adriana, but two paces back. Dryson to her right and Alfredo on the left. Adriana spoke to the group

'Back on earth, in answer to the question just made, we have,' Captain Dryson and Alfredo, received a slight head movement one to the other from Adriana before she continued.

'Established continuation of automata activity, to provide food production, and distribution. Previously Quadrant forces, were unaware of any absence of human leadership, because we maintained holographic representation, after departure. Higher officials, in each quadrant sector, and Fit for Life directors, have been informed of the true situation. Widespread panic would have occurred without intervention, you will understand.' A rhetorical statement, but applauded by Jeb and a few in the group immediately below the stage. Adriana now turned to Lara, Jeb and James and said,

'Can you leave the stage please for a moment I'll need extra space.'

'Are we to have visitors?' Asked Jeb, as the three got to their feet.

'Yes, that is our intention,' replied Adriana. Lara turned

to James

'Where are the display banners?

'Off stage, out the back.' These were two blue and yellow Fit for Life banners of an athlete running attached either on, pedestals that made them stand out vertically. James kept these in a haversack, for conference events and brought them to Mars. It would have been protocol to display these banners with quest visitors.

'I'll fetch them,' he said. It was unlikely extra-terrestrial visitors would in any way be impressed by a banner display or for that matter a Fit for Life conference, but routine earth procedures helped maintain a needed sense of togetherness. Routine and ritual having always been a part of human society

'Yes, if you don't mind,' said Lara. It was Jeb, who called down to where Heidi, Annette and Jo were sat with Mario and Ana.

'You kids give us a hand, will you?' Within a few minutes the groups chairs and table were cleared. Significantly, light across the capsule's auditorium dimmed. James, and Jeb were now in the audience and Lara had joined Lydia. There was quiet save for the live fluid within the capsule's double shell that made a low swishing sound as it harvested information from earth and space and absorbed sun energy. Quiet, that is before Captain Dryson detailed Alfredo to remove Adriana's throne-like chair from the stage. Then that low intensity whir started with each automaton's movement. When, Adriana next addressed the group, Captain Dryson was positioned at stage left of Adriana and Alfredo stage right. She began by saying,

'We understand how challenging your stay on this planet has been, but now there are plans to return to earth.

A group, involved with R &D and others are to stay, but this unit can be sustained without human presence. It's the Galactic Forces intention to develop an atmosphere suitable for earth biological presence outside of the main capsule, then this planet will become an attractive place for settlers from earth, we believe.'

'Mistress Adriana,' said, Captain Dryson.

'What is it Dryson?' eyes flashed annoyance at the interruption.

'A Galactic Force representative has entered this planetary complex, and requires to meet with you. Here to give holographic jurisdiction back to the earth planet for further development of its political and economic pathways.'

'Only holographic presence?'

'It wishes to be first here in holograms of characters and influences from earth history to talk to both you and those in this group?'

'What characters?' At this point Alfredo came in.

'Might I select these Empress Adriana. There are several which I follow from archive access to digital human record. Alfredo was more inclined to the social and communicative side of affairs, certainly than Captain Dryson.

'More able to entertain, than when just facts were presented.'

'Facts get to the truth, I cannot see the point,' said Captain Dryson.

'I'm happy with that. And that is all that matters,' replied Adriana. Their audience warmed to the idea. Evident by one from the group calling out,

'Let Alfredo have a say.'

'If you must. There are more important matters I need to deal with. One moment.'

'One moment.' A few seconds past, whilst Captain Dryson accessed earlier data.

'Yes, I understand,' he said. 'We will do that afterwards.'

'Do what Dryson?' demanded Adriana.

'You are to have full capabilities re -instated for the return to earth for group members.'

'We're to go back,' could be heard repeated from the audience arena'

'That's good,' said Adriana. 'But which status is to visit?'

'It is XP200. Permission has been given to enter this planetary system. To re-build biological structure in planets and create atmosphere, is a speciality, but first wishes to give an overview of earth and its ability to self-sustain.' At this point yellow and green plumes of intense light appeared on either side of the stage.

'We will need to leave Mistress Adriana,' said Captain Dryson, to give entities space.

'We'd better go then, hadn't we,' Adriana replied. A whirr from both Dryson and Alfredo started as they moved to the short stairway left of stage. Alfredo remained on the top step to facilitate transformation to the historical person of choice, whilst a third red plume arrived where Adriana previously stood centre stage.

Chapter 11

Alfredo chooses visitors, from earth history

SECONDS AFTER, A RED PLUME arrived, to flare inches above the central stage floor. A mixture of purple strands of light could be seen within the red. This meant that connectivity was maintained with XP1 and communication channels would be open. This understanding known to Adriana, Captain Dryson and Alfredo, but none of the Fit for Life party assembled. Alfredo, executed a bow. To which Adriana called out,

'Get on with it.' Murmur from the group, farther back into the audience could have been that of disapproval. There was affection for Alfredo, in that he would always explain what was happening and showed interest in their lives, as compared with Captain Dryson and Adriana, who maintained an aloofness. Unfortunately, often a necessary requirement where leader or leaders might make necessary demands that would be countered, should there be over familiarity. Visionary ideas and need for rapid action in the event of sudden circumstance change can lead to need for pragmatic, immediate decision making. There can be, an almost inevitable divergence of view, between the empowered and those who oppressed where they lacked resource to counter attack argument. Adriana's choice to remain materialized in human form, limited previous but news of reinstatement gave opportunity to regain empowerment. A situation, like that of a caged eagle confined, allowed to fly free. Impossible, though, to transfer with any certainty, actual human consideration of compassion, into an advanced life form, previously, unfamiliar with humans. This single factor, of whether there was compassion, was always likely to be a difficult proposition for humans to square with. Alfredo answered Adriana's demand of "Get on with it,"

'I will, my empress and ruler of our existence.' (Alfredo, ever aware of the emblem worn of absolute power toward his existence embodied in Adriana, controller of an automata's world, at the behest of the Galactic Force) Connectivity, like, an unbreakable silver thread which crossed frontiers vast oceans of space; Adriana was formed through the Galactic Force. Even, Captain Dryson who might feign a detachment from absolute control, was aware that if he crossed Adriana, his automata extreme status could be taken away by Galactic Force's decision to deselect his role of overall automata module control. Yes, Dryson and Alfredo were the automata able to take charge of the reinstatement of Adriana back into full galactic utterance, but any deviation from instructions would lead to executive power transference to a grade lower than theirs. A super plus, which might see Zita, for example, in a super plus category of executive capability, even though an earth developed automata. James would be amazed at this!

'Empress, my Captain and group members of Fit for Life representation, here on planet Mars, let me introduce a first visitor of choice for historical narrative and viewpoint. A character who was recreated to represent those oppressed down centuries of human activity? Within the spectrum of green out of legend and story the originator has chosen to appear for us. Behold before you now – Robin Hood of Locksley. This person asked to be addressed with title, because of association of place in his once earthly spectrum.'

At this point the red plume with purple inset moved above the stage, like a commanding presence and the green plume moved centre stage. There it remained and out stepped a figure in Lincoln green.

Imagery redolent of the person known as Robin Hood, formatted into legend down many earth centuries. A spirit flowed through re -invention which often paralleled the mores of the century or age. This person representative in a resplendent green that drew gasps from the group. A vibrancy associated with that seasonal depth given on earth when summer foliage is at its height. A reminder and incentive to be back on the home planet. Green of the tunic contrasted with a brown sword scabbard and shouldered quiver of arrows. A long bow held in left hand, taller than figure before them. This Robin Hood's first words were,

'Greetings to you of a distant future, that I could never have imagined. My language is similar to yours and has been adapted to be of your understanding, but am aware that generations upon generations have advanced ability far beyond those of us who had mainly a forest and what it offered for our survival and homes. That you in our hearts and minds are peoples who care for an order of forest and plant growth and have elevated the potential of trees beyond their natural regeneration on your known earth. We see from afar, but treasure still, a natural order that the seasons give to a planet that was once ours to share. We've been shown tree development for other purposes and understand how their roots emit into rivers, substance for shell growth, in sea fish. An integration and mix of all, natural process.

Where, we're concerned about oppression your group experienced on earth, recognition is given to those who experience tyranny from – powerful rulers. Now, taken from your birth home you should return with vigour to install fairness and justice through truth and fair minded-ness toward earth populations. But, from deep annals of knowledge Alfredo has revealed, before our visit, under-standing that Quadrant force leaders are situated for return. It is imperative that you are first back on earth to build empowerment for nation and cultural groups, across earth regions. Within, group entity we have brought regard and wishes for those who were once stalwart friends in many centuries past.' At this point, a woodland landscape back-ground developed around this figure in Lincoln Green. Numerous figures, attired in green, but without swords and arrow. quiver or long bow stood and knelt around this re-imagined figure from history – Robin Hood.

Within a swirled mist, above the stage, an earth, appeared, in rotation. Robin, withdrew an arrow and set it within his long bow. Turned, to sight toward this earth miniature.

'We wish safe passage. Follow this arrow, that describes to those, who watch, of your return. With this, the bow was drawn back. Its arrow released. For a moment, figures of well-wishers stayed in view, before they faded into the green plume. Robin Hood, re-energized in imagined appearance, turned back toward the Mars group. Bowed, before he too disappeared, into the ether. Not everyone, knew of this, folklore hero, from bygone years. All, clapped though, in appreciation, for powerful evocation of love, for their home planet. Alfredo, turned toward Adriana;

'Continue...Wait!' How many more have you found Alfredo from this planets' history?

'Two, most excellent Empress. One is a traveller or was once, across this planets' seas. Another a mystical spirit who wishes to talk from within the planet's being.

'There is important business to attend to, other than this entertainment.'

'It is understood. We can feel energy developing between planet Mars and planet earth, even, from our first visitor. Captain Dryson supported Alfredo's view with a nod of head.

'Yes, it is true, the vibrations of intensity are lifted. This will assist with gravitational force to make the flight of the rockets back to earth more effective.' Rippled talk spread through the group with mention of earth return.

Chapter 12

Alfredo brings forward a second visitor

'Now,' SAID ALFREDO, HIS VOICE competed with whirring noise, made from movement, as he returned to the stage's topmost step. Alfredo continued,

'Now, we have a traveller from later in earth history.' Not, you understand as a role model. More, that of, an adventurous character embodiment. For he was, at a time, when many peoples were enslaved, to enrich European powers of that era. Evil centuries, where enslavement, built wealth and subjugated noble peoples, in other countries and continents. This individual, was said to have continued a game of bowls before repelling an invading force, but he was also known to countenance enslavement. Born into a world that subjugated people, to amass wealth. Abolition of slavery, in 1865, did not immediately bring true freedom. Minds, hearts, displayed behaviour, in words, actions, behaviour which would not totally release, racial subjugation, even as late as 2020. Remember, that this character had flaws, which belonged to a period in history, and beyond. Alfredo, lifted a metallic articulated hand toward the yellow plume. Out of the plume first appeared a drum with heraldic symbols. Behind a figure in armour began to emerge. At which James said "Elizabethan," out loud, which caused Lara to follow with,

'– twenty first century?'

'No sixteenth!' James, replied in emphatic manner, which suggested that everyone should know that armour had ceased to be worn, in battle, by the time, of a second British queen. Breast plate armour covering upper body, was in black, with gold scrolled decoration. A stocky bearded figure stood before them, whilst left hand, grasped the mid-part of a scabbarded sword. Before speaking, he let go of the sword and raised both arms, as if to inspect scroll worked armour and dress.

'Yes, me lovers this'll do for Francis. Bess would've me, in a goodly armour to go to a watery grave. Not that Captain's armour they put me in.

'It is to your liking?' Enquired Alfredo.

'But where's me ship then?' replied this figure from Elizabethan time of exploration and conquest.

'That will follow. You agreed to talk with our group?' said Alfredo.

'That I did and will, when you've given my demands.' A hand reached out and fingers tapped across the drum's skin, which seemingly, on its own accord, developed a deep roll, which threatened toward very high volume, before, this apparitional figure, who purported to be Francis Drake, withdrew hand and fingers to shout,

'AVAST,' which made the drum go quiet, but also quietened those around. This creation from deeper realms continued with,

'Now, could first you give me like sound of a good breeze in the 't gallants' and the creak of a sturdy mast, and I'll begin?'

'Yes, yes, but then begin if you please... sir.' Alfredo,

noted Adriana's finger pointed toward the Time Taken Clock[1] which jumped completion time, that instant, the drum began to beat. Alfredo, perhaps now in reconsideration of choice, as a following with this sixteenth century, verbose figure, raised metallic arm and waved from figure to audience.

'Will you ...? Alfredo emphasised this requirement, by directing his sculpted mechanical eyes and head toward his senior automata Captain Dryson

'Will you? Can you please? Captain Dryson, access appropriate background sound?'

'Of course,' replied Dryson. It seemed as if Alfredo needed to reach out for emotional security to help control an entity that was more dominating than expected. Yes, Dryson was titled with that of a captain, but this former sea Captain personality was in a wholly different league! Almost immediately, the auditorium was filled with sounds like that of a powerful wind surge, together with repetitive thumping, back and forth, like that of wind pressure against sail. Then a discernible creak that might come from a tree mast embedded in the keel of a ship. An intermittent splattered sound, reminiscent of spray on an

---

1 Footnote: The Time Taken clock is a device which first appears in *Galactic Mission*. It enables connection between a viewer, who can silently ask, through mind communication, for an accurate time completion of a specific event. Originally designed to analyse incoming data to alert about cyber-attacks, but also able to compute, for individual viewer, when requested of its clock, an accurate time for an event end. The Taken Machine identifies delays which arise to thwart an original set time ending Event end, as understood, would then display a jump forward to a new completion time or conversely backwards should it be an earlier completion. A lengthy description for a self-revelatory named machine!

open wheelhouse deck. Then the groups second visitor to the Mars main capsule started to speak, once more.

'Ah, you've captured how that it was. My voice will fight the elements surround, but then I'll grasp to mind, all that is of most import.' To meet more directly with his audience, which might have been a crew below awaiting orders from a sea Captain. This second visitor let go of held drum strop and stepped forward to give advice.

'Ye'll not known, perhaps, how 'tis a ship is rescued, save by divine mercy from the likely swallow of raged wind and sea that will oft take no prisoners. Yet, I've been shown how tyrannical power has imprisoned those on earth to do their will with no regard for all other that not obey its demand to control all. Peoples were enslaved across the globe to do the will of mighty power be it Britannia or others, but now I see that the bounteousness of mother earth is there to be shared. I was careless in my day for other than a successful raid or conquest of a Spaniard brig, but wish to be with you when your quest is to save all that makes the earth so pleasant for man, creature, plant on land or sea. Yes, I was ill-regarded by the vanquished Spaniards in my day, but I saw that freedom would be lost if we did not fight to secure our territory and a little more. Yet, there were critics on English soil, and jealous feel, that secured Francis blessings of liege Queen Bess. ...But 'tis enough of me 'tis to your future and that globe I did once navigate right round, that I'm here to talk and recommend.' This figure from the past stopped for a moment and appeared to be looking around and above before continuing.

'It's like some great cathedral that we're in. But you said, we'd be upon a planet in the heaven's?' The visitor turned to address Alfredo.

'That's right Sir Francis. Our group is in a dome built to

create earth-like gravitation and air to breathe. We selected suitable fauna and material that would grow food from a seed bank. Supplies are loaded aboard our ships to enable journeys to distant planets that support life.

'Tis, invention beyond my imaginings. I know mostly seas on earth, but did also did do civic work and know in this, that you will be, so involved. My dialect and speech I will attune now to your ears and this is my message –

"I ask your courage to do what is right for the safety of all on earth. Alfredo, has shown how Quadrant hierarchy prepare to return. You must be first there to warn each area, it must elect from its people leaders that speak, for each and every one and not just that powerful group. In centuries past, my drum it was said would beat its message when attack threatened the isles I knew. But now it's for the earth. I will be there for you and warn when all is not well." With this last statement the apparitional Sir Francis stepped back and placed hands and fingers on the drum skin, again. A more rapid beat came into the capsule surround, but then both drum and entity, went quiet and were re-absorbed within the plume.

Chapter 13

Adriana resisted

'AND FOR YOUR NEXT AND "final," choice,' Adriana called across to Alfredo.

'A mystical embodiment from inner earth that has visited to display a leader fit to save a Kingdom, my Empress, as was once known on this planet earth. Also, Empress this will open access for your Galactic family to communicate.'

'Good.' We will break for fifteen earth minutes. The plumes can remain until, then can't they?' Adriana asked Alfredo.

'Yes, Empress, they're locked into the planet's orbit with direct link to Galactic Forces. We have no control. They will leave only after you're reinstated to travel to and from the Force, and then to any planet in your adopted planetary system.

'Good, then I will be back stage' This was a cue for a fleet of hover trays to swoop, in front of the stage, from upper reaches of the capsule to clustered tables below, to provide refreshments. James was sat opposite to Lara when Captain Dryson approached their table.

'What is it Dryson?' Lara addressed the automata just like Adriana would and was treated with equal respect.

'Mistress Lara. It is that Adriana, most excellent ruler

of these planets wishes to speak with James. It is before re
-instatement to full embodiment of galactic ability.

'James, you'd best not keep your partner waiting.' Lara
called across the table to him.

'It's a business partnership,' said James.

'Are you saying it's none of our business? It was Captain
Jeb who joined the conversation.

'Could be,' said James, who wanted to keep them
guessing and anyway, if it was his personal life that they
wanted to know about it was none of their business
anyhow.

'Where's Adriana-Dryson?' Asked James.

'Empress Adriana is back stage in the main dressing
room.' The theatre was a recreation of a proscenium arch
theatre with back stage dressing rooms, plus an entrance
and exit at the rear, into and out of the main capsule.

'You can go through the stage curtains. The main
dressing room is down the right corridor, it says ...'

'Yes, yes I know the way.'

'We want you back James, when Adriana's finished
with you,' said Lara.

'I'm not planning to go anywhere – on my own.' James
got to his feet and climbed the stairs.

He was keen to get a closer look at the plumes.

'Do not touch the plumes,' called out Captain Dryson.'
They destroy anything that touches their aura.'

'Alright, I wasn't planning to,' said James. Although
he might just have done. As he walked between the green
and red with purple plume, he heard the voice of a woman,
call out. "It is to return. No more will it be hidden."
Presumably, a new next visitor was waiting within the
plume, so to speak. James, intrigued by what Alfredo
might have brought from another time dimension entered

darkness, in the inner corridor, save for a middle row of spotlights, which shone up from the floor. Sufficient to illuminate names on doors, but not much else. The first door said "Make up Room,' the second "First Aid and Stretcher," and finally Main Dressing Room. The door opened. Adriana, must have heard his footsteps. In the short time between leaving the main auditorium Adriana had changed into a green dress, with wide opening sleeves, and plunging neckline. Gold necklace displayed a golden disc model of the sun from which eight planets, represented by a precious stone were attached by golden thread. James, perhaps wondered whether the gold and precious stones were detected and mined by automata, since their arrival. Adriana's first words were,

'I put this dress on for you.' James was most likely impressed, but said,

'It's nice, but you needn't have bothered.'

'Look James! Lara, isn't able to offer you the power and position that I can offer.'

'What makes you think that's what I want and not you?'

'You'll have me. We can be together and visit other planets.'

'That's it. I'll leave earth and all the sense of being a person on the planet.'

'We could return. That ability for my movement between worlds will soon be returned. You can be with me on those visits and re-visit your friends. Otherwise, I will be alone within a complexity which is exhilarating, but I feel, and understand how it is for your species of earth. I will feel absence, if you are not with me when re-instatement is made. Adriana, at this point opened her arms and James moved forward and they kissed, but only

69

momentarily before parting. He felt the taut firmness of her body beneath her dress. Eyes, seemingly filled with pleading, but James was unable to move to commitment. Their time on Mars was not one of togetherness. He lived in a chalet within the complex, which brought him into closer contact with Lara, not Adriana. The personality he met in Adriana was not that of Lara's, although physically they were as twins. Sexual allure yes, that remained, but now away from earth, so much about their personal relationship, now in memory, found no appeal, with a nature that was intrinsic to Adriana – threatening; particularly now, that this creature was about to regain position of total power, over earth and planets.

Adriana's pleading eyes, seemed genuine, but that could have been guile. James resisted any desire to kiss her with passion, whilst his hand enveloped beneath her long fair hair, before he moved back from their embrace.

'It is not farewell James; you will still work with me to partner our project on earth return?'

Adriana turned to pick up a hair brush, with a smile, where lip movement reflected back from the dressing room mirror. It was not for James to know, but perhaps she'd achieved what was required from the meeting?

'I acquiesce Adriana, in the interests of the group.'

'Just acquiesce? I can hope for more can I not?

'Not as it stands.'

'Ah, I feel there is what is called wriggle room, though.' Adriana, smiled mischievously, and seemed undaunted by the situation. She replaced the brush on the table, took hold of James's arm and kissed his cheek, before saying.

'We must return to see what Alfredo has to offer for a final visitation. This is not goodbye James. A pathway is open, even when I reinstate. We met first when I visited in the Galactic paradigm. I know much more and your position, I understand. Please return to the group and I will follow.' The romantic nature of this encounter changed to that of operational business, as if a light was switched off.

Chapter 14

Alfredo's Final choice

VOICE CHATTER DIED DOWN WHEN Adriana re
-entered through stage curtains, no longer in a green dress,
but dressed in more formal work attire of a senior representative of the Fit for Life group, namely that of a navy
top with Fit for Life logo, skirt, matched with knee length
boots made of a material compacted from grasses grown
in the agricultural sites of the Martian extended capsules.
Identically dressed to Lara, save for the necklace band
which displayed precious stones for individual planets,
whose central sun disc held out golden threads not only
a depiction of the actual sun's hold, but also prescient
omnipotence of its necklace wearer. Each plume, of light,
in turn, appeared to bend, as if to bow when Adriana
walked across. Captain Dryson and Alfredo were stood
either side at the foot of the stairway. When she stopped
to make an announcement, which was,

'You may continue, Alfredo, when everyone is settled.'

Hover trays were in attendance above. Ready to amplify
and interpret.

'Thank you, Empress Adriana.'

Adriana walked down from the stage and joined a
table, to the right of James, where Lara was, with son Matt,
Lydia, with Elsie, and Captain Jeb Lucas. Mario and Ana

were on an adjacent table with Annette, Jo and Heidi. A remainder of the group, in the auditorium, sat mainly at tables of four.

'Visitor, please reveal your presence,' announced Alfredo. Both the green and yellow plumes moved out of view into the wings. There was the sound of flowing water, which appeared to arrive, from above full height of the curtained space, whilst the red and purple plume subsided. There developed a waterfall cascade in hologram with trees, shrubs and boulders on both sides. Moss-covered boulders, showed, amidst the waterfall. Spontaneously, at stage front, a fast-running stream. This caused the audience to lean back, some even get to their feet, although the rush of water which tumbled over the stage ended above the auditorium in a foam of misted spray. Twisted patterns could be seen, amidst the water swirl on stage. Made it appear more like a flow of molten metal, than just water. Another boulder rose up midstream. Each side white, sprayed, from flowed water. Then, an extended slender arm held a sword aloft, before a woman's head and shoulders, appeared. Before the sword arm was lowered. She threw the sword upwards, whilst hair in tightly plaited tresses, danced about her neck. Golden handle and silver blade flashed, as if caught in sunlight, twirled upwards, before its tip caught in the rock above. Water didn't appear to penetrate a six pleated translucent dress. Embroidered replicas of the sword decorated it from waist to ankle. Eight replica, dagger sized swords embroidered the fabric around the bodice area. It made the young woman appear unconnected with the water and more like an apparition. Hand and footholds enabled a climb to the top of the boulder, where she stood next to the embedded sword. Her first words as she stood atop the boulder with hands on waist, were.

'Bleeding heck, Alfredo, my category is lake not waterfall! This waterfall area is more nymphs and woodland territory.' Alfredo was not overly disturbed by this outburst from his chosen visitor.

'You inhabit this earth's watery region and not just lakes and "really," this vista is of more attraction to my group. Our group will be more interested in what you have to say in these surrounds.' Certainly, the view of a waterfall cascade and the green of trees, moss and plants gave powerful evocation of earth's natural world. A lake on its own could have been a bit bleak and forbidding. For this view Alfredo received unexpected support from Adriana.

'Lady of the Lake, you have been given a good setting to reveal what you have to tell the group, continue please.' Awareness of Adriana's attendance gave a rapid adjustment from peevishness to positivity with removal of hands from hips and a curtsey adjoined with a smile.

'Your supreme excellency from the galaxies, it is as you wish. I understand the need to support this earth group, who can with your especial presence do much to rectify the turmoil that I have seen, in past centuries visited on earth's natural order by discoveries that have threatened the well-being of the biosphere...'

'Continue! Lady of the Lake, with relevance to the topic of earth return! Adriana interrupted. You are now linked to the Galactic Force, I understand. Are you not?' It was Captain Dryson who replied.

'Lady of the Lake is a compilation of spirit and legend prominences, from earth history, who has recognized urgency to rejuvenate the human species and remedy dangerous activity. This appeal arrives from within the biospheres of many natural influences. Not just from human appeal. Empress, a call was made two centuries ago, in human time.'

'Then, make your address relevant and not too wordy then – Lady of the Lake,' Adriana replied,

'Of course, your soon to be supreme excellency, once more. We have been calling and are ready to re-engage after your excellency has full Galactic empowerment. I request to differ on the compilation statement. We update to "I" for every century and "I" am the Lady of the Lake for this 22nd century.' Adriana just replied with the word, "continue," before turning to Captain Dryson and saying,

'Can you intercept to allow Galactic import?'

'Yes, that is possible. My raised hand will end the talk. Lady Vivian is in rather talkative mode.' The Lady of the lake, started her supportive conversation to the group, with,

'Greetings to you all, from Mother Earth, on this smaller planet.' Lady Vivian curtseyed and on rising, enabled a willow flower basket to appear in the crook of her arm, filled with red and white rose petals, which she scattered. Within seconds the rock she stood on was carpeted with petals. Rose scent wafted through the auditorium. A tantalizing reminder of earthly fragrance.

'That's better, I feel more able to relax for this talk. I would rather that it was apple blossom, but never mind. My purpose is to heal impurities on earth. Not just, bodies and minds of inhabitants. Yes, you are all far away, but I journey to be with you. A corridor of transmission was opened by Galactic Force on its first arrival, for enabled travel, from earth to here. It will remain open in assistance, for your return and I can stay, but momentarily. A new season of spring, in the northern hemisphere, on earth, requires my presence and help. In particular, where water dominates in lakes and inland water flow. I am that healing presence to lead away from winter into spring.' Captain Dryson whispered to Adriana,

'I understand what you mean my Empress.' But Lady Vivian moved to more meaty information.

'This sword.' She placed a small hand on the sword's handle, and stopped the quiver, caused from where its tip first embedded in the rock.

'This sword is Excalibur, which in times past gave power, to whoever was fit to possess it. A sword with magical properties. Now it is refashioned to take on the power of darkness once again. Its holder will be there when you require rescue from mortal danger on return to earth. I am a caring earth goddess and have responded to the call from our earthly biosphere and from that of the approach from galactic travellers. The sword I will return to earth domain to a boulder now submerged. This place will release Excalibur. When you see the sword raised skywards it will forewarn you of danger and confute your enemy.'

At this point, it was Adriana who raised her hand and Captain Dryson prompted Alfredo to bring this visitor talk to a conclusion. Immediately, his voice called out with,

'Thank you earth goddess; we are appreciative of your visit and care for the group. We're receiving input from galactic visitors. Would you now make the link?'

'If you wish,' there was annoyance in the voice at the termination of her speech, but the message was revealed about the properties of Excalibur and symbolism going forward. This goddess figure from mythological past times, with both hands, removed sword from rock and held it aloft. Whereupon both sword, goddess and background vanished to be replaced by a tall male figure in Fit for Life dress style of tunic and trousers. At either side two automata of humanoid replication to that of Captain Dryson and Alfredo, but instead of black metallic casing theirs was more, translucent green, intermingled with red.

'XP200,' announced Captain Dryson to Adriana, before he turned to address this new arrival.

'Greetings and welcome to you our new Galactic over lord for Mars. You've chosen a group member of African ancestry. A chosen person from within our group, named Alexander.' Niobe, his partner, who sat next to him, grabbed his arm and said.

'Alex, they've chosen you.' Niobe was impressed but Alexander perhaps less so, because he said,

'They could've asked.'

'Don't be silly, you're recognized. We're part of something bigger.'

'Maybe. If you don't mind like two of me.' There discussion stopped when they realized others nearby had realized how Alexander had been cloned like Lara before. Alexander said,

'I'll play him at table tennis. See if he measures up...' Before a shush came from tables either side, as Alexander's look alike started to speak.

'My galactic status is XP200, as has been announced. Greetings to you, Adriana, Empress of all planets, which circle the sun, including this one named Mars. Congratulations that you have saved its neighbour earth from destruction and I address, you the Fit for Life Group and yes, Alexander we recognized your contribution to the groups research and development progress whilst on Mars with botanical growth rejuvenation project. We can be partners going forward. My presence here to "green," this planet, which was a fertile and habitable planet in previous eons, and yes, my galactic expertise concurs with your interests. Joined with me are two automata developed for earth return. My role is to re-invigorate this Planet for future settlement. My chosen name is Antar.

Antar, as of the star Antares. Before anything else, Adriana my arrival and first purpose is, with your two automata's assistance, to complete reinstatement of your full status. A corridor will then be open and you can revisit earth, in either holographic or cloned human form, prior to rocket re-assimilation of your group on earth.' Adriana smiled and with her two automata, Captain Dryson and Alfredo, one either side made for the stage, to join XP200.

At a previous all group meeting an announcement was made as to the names of those chosen to make up the return earth party. It was decided that four groups of twenty were needed to meet requirements. Determined, in part by the fact, that mothers with young children were prioritized. Earth was the home planet for everyone, save for Adriana and background appreciation for earth, was felt to be necessary, until independent adult choices could be made. The Fit for Life group, included couples with children. All escapees from a world threatened by comet destruction and totalitarianism. On return the plan would be to recover autonomy for state groups across the world, with assistance from Galactic Force now returned to the outer reaches of the solar system.

Places, beyond those prioritized were chosen, alternately by Alfredo and Captain Dryson, from a revolved drum, with numbered participant tickets. Both android automatons were considered impartial observers. Part of Mars evening entertainment centred around the employment of the random drum selector to choose an evening's social activity. James, having located this drum idea from an archive, which displayed a game show that produced, randomly, sequenced numbers and matched prize winners, way back in the twentieth century. With Antar and both new galactic entities on stage, it was James who called out.

'What are their names? The new Automata.'

Antar, turned first to the automata on his right and a female voice was heard to say

'We've chosen names from earth past. My name is Thea.' The other said,

and mine is Athena.'

Chapter 15

Adriana and plans for earth return

RESPONSES BETWEEN THE TWO GALACTIC entities XP100 and now XP200 were now superimposed, as it were into human construct. Previously, data flowed between them with relevance to their special fields of expertise. Now they were formed into materialized beings, and bipedal body type they were enabled auditory communication with eyes to absorb feelings and emotions. Previously of a defined polarity of expertise and no sexual reproductive reference, they came together now as man and woman. XP200, or Antar made an immediate translation to the human male understanding, through revision first made by Adriana, in progress through to human species. Relevance of sexuality and at first shock, it could be said, that reproductive ability still existed within capabilities of the human frame.

Antar did not bow or defer in the manner of an Automata, but reached out his hand which Adriana held, whilst eyes met. It's not recorded which one made the first move, but Antar kissed her cheek which was proffered when he drew Adriana near. They let go of hands and were now between two automata on stage, to face the group audience. A sound, like that of rushing wind could be heard, as an interpretation was made, in varied languages into minds of those present. Hover tray communication bypassed with ascendant force field and dominant galactic input on to Mars, through the solar system. A message from the Galactic Force began with,

"It is determined in this space of planetary disposition, and planetary solar system that XP100, missioned in the role name, Adriana be granted full re-instatement to Galactic provenance through the arrival of XP200. Antar, is to augment, further development on this planet named Mars. A return enabled for XP100 to earth resolution, in holographic or human clone portrayal, as events require." After this lengthy statement the next words seemed very simplistic.

'XP100 and XP200 are to hold hands. Automata you will receive algorithm data apposite to fulfil commands, now given.' This message was voiced only to Adriana and Antar, whilst the group audience witnessed, holding of hands, followed by switch for Adriana's human body to holographic form. This followed immediately. It was Adriana who spoke.

'Welcome to Antar. This is from one, who now has presence in dual domain. Information has been given that Quadrant leaders and their followers, on the Moon know that comets trajectories toward earth have been diverted. It's vital that we return to rally support across world populations. We will soon need to exit this planet. There will be a platform of opportunity to arrive back on earth, before Quadrant can regain control. Antar will remain on Mars with Captain Dryson and Alfredo to monitor all systems and work with those who remain to gain understanding of Martian atmosphere, through research and development. To bring forward colonization, with earth fauna, fish and animals, with increased human occupational capacity. I need to leave for the Galactic command force to further assess earth's situation. On my return, those chosen to leave Mars must be prepared. The hologram representing Adriana vanished and a screen text appeared which gave an account of the situation, on earth, since the departure of Quadrant hierarchy to the effect -that, after an initial state of panic, life returned to its previous rhythm. The sun, after all continued to rise and set. Seeds germinated within the fertile conditions engendered through automata nurture and creation of productive environment. Be it, in adapted tree root deep access of water, for food type crop, or new varieties of soil root crop production.

Further development of inner-city crop growth continued alongside solar energy production to harvest and store energy not required in water elevation for future hydro-electric production flow, in winter months, across respective north and south hemispheres.

Before departure of Adriana's hologram, which denoted re-instatement to full potential and overall control of the solar planetary system these were the final words relayed by the Galactic Force.

'Earth automata in the four Quadrant capitals – New York, Beijing, Moscow and London have acknowledged that comet trajectories have been averted away from earth proximity. We may meet with resistance from those who will want to support the old regime on our return.'

Chapter 16

James with Mario

'**What does the future hold** for us?' I was with Mario after the meeting back in the sports and recreation section of the capsule. I'd challenged Mario to table tennis, not to seek revenge on his beating me previously, but more to sound out his take on the latest developments. Mario's table tennis improved after he enlisted help from the sports arena automaton coach. This automaton was able to slow return ball velocity and give Mario opportunity to build up technique, through practice. Mario, it must be said was more into physical sport, than I was. Already, my return serves were hitting the net before Mario scaled down his new found technique and allowed rallies to follow with chat about our situation.

'You mean the human race, I, guess...
James?'

'Yes and no,' I said. 'It's more about longer-term. How much control that there'll be over our existence with such dominance by machines and just us, still as cogs, in the machinery of Fit for Life. That's whether we're still wanted?'

'That's very bleak, James. Can't understand why you turned down that proposal from your replica boss. Talk about ultimate control and power.' I replied, with,

'Recognize my limitations Mario. Heavy hangs the head that wears the crown.'

'What the hell does that mean James?'

'It's a saying – goes way back when there were kings who made the decisions and then got blamed when things went wrong. Galactic Force is here now, but we were virtually, left on Mars to await re-engagement.'

'Yeah, but with state of art technology, beyond our know how.' We'd stopped playing and were talking across the net to one another when I said,

'I'm being shown around an interior part of one of their space ships by Alfredo, later.'

'You are? How's that going to happen James? There's been a repulse shield around the site from arrival build, he said, whilst, placing the table tennis ball under the bat on the table.

'Alfredo will lift it temporarily.'

'Does best buddy Adriana know about this?'

'Adriana, is not best buddy. I'm still part of the human race Mario,' I said. 'I've only gone along with the notion of partnership. It seemed safer at the time.'

'Yeah, and don't I feel sorry for you hanging out with that bombshell.'

'What do you mean, you've got Ana. You're an item, shall I tell her...'

'No,' but it sets you apart from everyone. You do see that James?' Anyhow, how about me partnering with you to view inside the rocket James?'

'If Alfredo agrees, yes.'

'And Adriana?'

'It would have been sanctioned by Adriana in the first place, don't you think?'

Chapter 17

Visit to space ship

IT WAS TWO DAYS, THAT'S in Martian time, since my last meet up with Mario, when we, that's Mario and myself were allowed an appointment, with Alfredo, to visit the space ship platform are. Placed, two hundred metres away from the recreation area, in a second tier, above the main capsule, each of the two space ships held in cradle like structures. A ship could be elevated within ten seconds, whilst the egg-shaped protective shield above withdrew its cover simultaneously. Platform protection material was of honeycomb texture five metres deep. Heat absorbed by the material generated into electrical energy. I'd attended lectures conceived for scientific members of the group, whilst we'd been located on the red planet. Layout was described, but in all honesty, I didn't believe earth scientists understood about how molecules and atoms were re-engineered to build new material, anymore than me. There was talk about re-engineering certain appliances constructed by the robots. Lectures were organized by automata. Designed purposely to give intermediary level interpretation for scientific members of our group. In particular , construction capsule build and capability.

These lectures and tutorials were to explain methods

of construction to house group members; plant insect breeding unit, to meet protein requirement; solar power assimilation; research facility; recreation equipment and the design of pod tunnels. One of which Mario and me were to enter for travel from the recreation area. Faux live entertainment, was available with virtual reality headsets. Where calm and relaxation might be found through music, these virtual reality systems could produce an effect to that of being on earth, because you could interact with scenery like a beach environment or scent the pollen of flowers. Avatars were on hand to talk with and answer questions. I wanted to know more about hybrid sail craft that had been developed, which doubled up as low fly airships when sea weather conditions deteriorated. An avatar, in virtual reality was helming one of these craft, when he was relieved of his position, by another attired in Elizabethan naval dress.

'See James, I've transformed into the guise of that Drake, person.' It was Zita. There was, I believing that it was only Mario and me in the pod, until now.'

'Your covers blown then; they know you're here then?'

'No, not necessarily James and any how I just appear as a malignant escaped hover tray automaton.'

'I'd go with the malignant bit.'

'Very unfair James. You could hurt my feelings, if I didn't understand your way of expression. You approve my re-interpretation of our visitor? Couldn't resist when you said there was a chance for a guided tour of a space ship'

'You'll be spotted though.'

'Not if you put your virtual earth display, on standby before you leave the pod. There'll be enough formatted material, for Zita, to be like an invisible eye in a wall painting.'

'And if I don't?'

'You will. You'll need my record and information analysis for future reference. There will be capability, within the space ship, which will not be acceptable to the human mind and physical dimension perspective.'

'And this will be understandable to you?' I asked.

'Zita exists, in part, at least, close to their appreciation of multi-layered interface. I don't want to appear a know all, when they're in ascendance above earth automata development.' I interrupted.

'Sorry Zita, you do want to appear super smart?'

'Your words not mine, James. I'm concerned about what might happen now you've gone off Adriana. That's really all.'

'You were happy with the proposition made then?'

'Not happy, but I would appreciate all that was on offer with regard to galactic knowledge and development in outer spheres and dimensions, beyond this galaxy, and immediate star systems.'

'No real concern for the earth then, or less significantly your companion to human assistance offered to me?'

'That would remain. You don't appreciate, James, my dialogue is constrained away from all earth automata. I feel like Robinson Crusoe now that I'm here.'

'My heart bleeds, for you, Zita. I'll put the virtual on standby, anyhow,' I said.

'That's really appreciated James. You'll not regret that decision, I'm sure.'

A green illuminated sign above Mario's head flashed "Arrival," and I switched the virtual set to stand by, before I replaced unit to holder. Mario, who was sat opposite did the same. Once the swing momentum from the cabled pod stopped, doors slid open. We stepped on to a disembarkation plate and were lowered into the vast domed cavern which housed the two space ships. Alfredo was just under two metres in height but appeared insect-like, between the two, now horizontally cradled space ships, whose material surfaces shimmered, emitting a display of power, like that of living creatures in the half light, like when you see a lion or tiger, even when at rest. We were nearly level with Alfredo when he gave an arm wave and head nod. With no visible face expression, impossible to know what this humanoid-like automata was feeling or thought. We awaited speech recognition. This followed.

'James, Mario welcome to the rocket enclosure.' This was said, in a way that a horse trainer might welcome you on a visit to thorough-bred horses.

'They've been re-configurated,' arms opened toward where the cylinder structures of the rockets stretched away either side of Alfredo.

'They are now named after you two. This one is Mario and the other James.'

'We're flattered I'm sure,' I said. Mario nodded in agreement, but he might only see this as an example of alien intervention and capture, to help keep us on side.

'James, is the one to leave with the group on return to earth, soon.'

'That means that you want me to stay does it?'

'No Mario, the space ships are just named after you two. It was my idea and the Empress agreed that they could be so named.'

'Big of Adriana,' Mario whispered. I'm not sure why he bothered to whisper, the sentiment would have been picked up by Alfredo. I calmed the situation by saying,

'No, we don't mind.' I wanted to view inside, because

on arrival the space ships were almost immediately cocooned above, where the main capsule build was, and no one had seen them since. On this Mars, first arrival, we were escorted out of the space ship almost immediately. Automata and robotic construction workers were placed on Mars by the Galactic Force before we landed and had already built a main capsule and made this habitable for our group's arrival. A configuration of materials that I knew nothing about. They defied physical laws, as understood on earth. Achieved by Adriana's, so called, family, which prepared Mars for our visit earlier.

Alongside the first rocket, named after me, was a gantry with a replication platform, similar to that for entry and exit to the pod. Alfredo, must have messaged instructions, at this point, because a wide screen supported by drone automata arrived, above the gantry, and appeared to merge with the side of the rocket.

'This is new for you?' said Alfredo. 'You were shown a disembarkation space on arrival, but not how it was made?' It was Mario who called out,

'How does that happen?' when the screen lit to reveal first an opaque plasma like swirl of material, which cleared into first translucent material then disappeared, to leave a rectangular opening, in the side of the rocket.

'There it is open for us to view,' said Alfredo.

'You've shown this happening. But not how?' Said Mario.

'One day, but it will need to be when you are further forward and able to more fully understand. Not just you two, but all who want to know. Shall we get aboard the platform?'

We let Alfredo step on first. In seeming contradiction to other advanced technology, platform-controlled rise was with a hand held tablet. All three of us were now on the railed platform. Apart from a slight hissing noise, from a conventional pressure system designed to raise the platform there was quiet in the vast hanger dome.

'You see,' said Alfredo. He raised his left black metallic arm upwards, as we approached the opened rocket entrance from ground level.

'You see the dome above.' When I'd looked, before all I'd been were aware of was a void of black that stretched high above and assumed that its inner structure would be black with perhaps strengthening bands or arches. It was Mario, who responded with a

'Wow.'

'It's a biological seed structure and designed to respond to the gaze or interest notice of other similar type.'

'Do you mean it recognizes us?' I said. The deep recess of the dome was now a deep yellow, teamed with what appeared to be green tadpole like creatures, which darted back and forth?'

'Yes, it is a life form,' said Alfredo, 'which has the ability to induce gravity on to a planet's surface. Within each space ship, there are seed pods that have hatched into structures above capsules and this dome. They're to give you earth gravitational force. It is able to recognize your biological need for a specific gravity.'

'And it knows who we are?' Asked Mario.

'Not individually, but it reads that you are a biological structure. Your eyes are like windows of recognition, for it to understand what your needs are. "Slow the platform, and increase to Mac 2, the gravity." commanded Alfredo.

My feet and legs instantly experienced that upward pressure from a lift which stops abruptly, with extra pressure exerted.

'Return to earth gravity stability,' said Alfredo. The lift continued its ascent and the pressure was removed.

'I guess it will eliminate gravity then.' Said Mario.

'Yes, when it opens and spreads its petal like cover it will supress gravity to assist with a rocket launch.' There was no time for any more questions since we'd arrived exactly level with the entry point.

This part I remembered. Inside the space ship displayed now closed, you could see, elaborate pod structures which hibernated each of us on our journey from earth to Mars. I remembered these being of a red colour, now they were blue/ green. Alfredo explained.

'You see they are now the colour of your earth for the return journey. It is also a more restful colour do you not think?' Mario came in here with,

'Can we get to see the propulsion units?'

'It is unattainable for you,' replied Alfredo. That area draws energy and existence from other dimensions. You cannot get near, nor the nose cone. I've a view panel for you to see cargo spaces and storage provision area. Also, craft, which have been designed for you to sell. We can show you this.

'To sell! To whom?' I asked.

Alfredo replied,

'We've not been entirely cleared with that of purpose,' a wordy transcript for the fact that we were told a lie about being given a tour of the ship.

'There are visitors due.'

Chapter 18

Explanations and Plans

JAMES AND MARIO WERE IN the mid-section of the rocket with Alfredo. A space large enough to accommodate at least one thousand passengers, within mounted hibernation pods. Each one, absorbed three metres of space and ran along inner walls. Five hundred on each side. Alfredo, was, in the midst of showing, James and Mario, on their tablet screens, layout of cargo holds, and their contents, beyond passenger area, when the platform outside could be heard journeying back from below.

'Our visitors have arrived and will be with us shortly,' Alfredo said.

'Visitors from some other time frame?' Asked Mario. A not unreasonable question to ask in consideration of Alfredo's previous selection of visitors for the group.

'It is not a secret. Empress Adriana wants key earth party members together to explain plans for earth return,' said Alfredo. Voices could be heard as the platform arrived. Adriana was heard to say.

'Antar will help explain plans, we have for earth return. It's better that we are together. away from the remainder of your group at this point.' Jeb's deeper voice replied with,

'I'll be happy to sleep in my old bed, if it's still there.' He spotted James and Mario,

92

'You two guys going ahead of us then?'

'No, Jeb we're just on a guided tour, but it's at an end by the looks of it,' said Mario.

'Ah, Empress we have prepared an area for your meeting,' Alfredo actioned light to shine in a break of travel pods. This, lit chairs, set in a circle to face the inner casing of the rocket. A blue misted screen strip lit, to show a view of the earth, from Mars. Awe, for the delicate, luminescent blue glow, quietened the group. Adriana looked around.

'Good. – James what we have to show everyone will interest you. A craft has been designed which will skim across surface waves and with waves too high, can also fly. Everyone please to sit and view the screen picture inside the cargo hold.'

Immediately, after the last person was sat down, picture screen switch, showed a cavernous space. Then a camera homed in on a Catamaran style craft, one hundred metres in length. Port holes ran along the visible hull and above this, a superstructure, set around two short but bulky masts. These were rigged with meshed sails. Adriana walked to the front with Captain Dryson and Alfredo and before sitting down said,

'Explain Dryson. You have interest in these earth propulsion machines.'

'Happy to do so, my Empress. First, may I say welcome to the rocket named James – Oh no, not just to James, but everyone.' Alfredo chipped in with,

'We, that's Captain Dryson and myself decided to name the space ships James and Mario. We hope you don't mind, we noticed how you give names to boats and other vehicles.'

'They don't mind,' said Adriana. To which James and Mario, nodded in agreement, whilst Annette said,

'Ship's usually have female names. Don't they?' Lara, then came in with,

'Carry on Dryson, if you want to name the rockets after James and Mario and they have no objection, then that's okay.'

'Quite, said Adriana. 'Now get on with the talk, Dryson.'

'Thank you, Empress and Mistress Lara,' but without saying, "before I was so rudely interrupted," instead shone a light from an extended metallic arm, to further illuminate the craft on screen display.

'This craft and three others have been developed from accessed ideas formed by James.' It was Jeb, who leant forward, to look at James, with raised eyebrows. Perhaps with concern for what else these automata had managed to access from his mind! Captain Dryson continued.

'Twin hull construction was decided on, because automata design team, decided this construction would give best sea surface speed. We will now show an overhead elevation.' The monitor camera within the space projected a downward view of the craft. Sails on both masts, were seen to be setting from an artificial breeze created. Then released to flap, whilst drawn into the interior of each bulky mast. Between each hull, a metallic scissor device drew the hulls together. Once both hulls were against the large centre bridge space, the main cabin deckhead opened, and guys or perhaps, more appropriately halyards from masts fore and aft, assisted to both lift out an aerodynamic tube. Before half inflation, fore ends of the twin hulls could be seen to lift from the cargo hold, but deflation brought the craft back to its former stable position on the space ships cargo deck.

'I've stopped it inflating further,' Said Captain Dryson.

At this stage, camera view altered to twin hull view, where turbo-engine outlets could be seen.

'Oxygen, is drawn from air around and pressure created. Electricity, is extracted from solar particles in sails to charge batteries, when the craft is a yacht, and from the aerodynamic balloon fabric when airborne. There is a top air speed of two hundred miles per hour, but only in quiet weather zones. Surface speed can be a little in access, of twenty knots. Sail ability allows access to harbours and air travel to inner cities, towns etc...

'That's neat,' said James.

'We're pleased that you approve of our rendition of your ideas.'

'Yes, thank you to both,' said Adriana, who with Antar got to her feet, in preparation to hold the floor. Lara, turned to James,

'That's just up your street isn't it, James. But where's this leading to?' The party were about to find out. Adriana and Antar, bathed in light, stood either side of the screen. A light behind switched off before Adriana started to talk.

'You arrived as an expeditionary force. Antar is to front remaining members of the group, here on Mars. A Galactic Force presence, soon, will allow us to give access to earth, as before. You and three other groups will return by rocket to undersea bases.'

'Other groups, how do you mean?' Asked Jeb.

'There're three more Air/Sea Skaters, like the one you've been shown. Antar has contacted Colonel Peters, on earth, and these sail/fly machines were built to display to the four main capital cities – London, New York, Beijing and Moscow. We made sure that all in the four groups were swimmers and each crew has at least one person with sea or flight background experience. More, will be explained, but Antar would like to tell you about the earth situation. Adriana stepped back, and Antar forward,

'Thank you, Empress, Adriana. Antar's selected voice was deep in tone and bounced out and beyond where they were all sat.

Firstly, I want to say how delighted that I have been chosen to remain here with the remainder of the expeditionary force. You are soon to leave for earth. All four craft will be stored to be assembled on arrival – I must ask. Are any one of you unhappy about travelling to London aboard one of these craft? They are to a high specification.'

'From where?' Asked Lara.

'Your space ship is to land, and enter the Atlantic Ocean miles seawards of the West African coast. You'll be able to practice sail and air skills aboard your craft, before you leave for London. Craft, that are smaller than the escape air ship, which carried your total group, away from danger on earth, but more versatile, as you can see. We will in turn meet here with the other groups to explain this plan. On earth, after the Quadrant hierarchy departed all systems in each capital control centre were set to lock and run.'

Group One's crew included with Athena and Thea – Lara, Matt, James, Mario, Ana, Heidi, Annette and Jo, with an additional twelve from out of the total eighty, chosen for the return to earth. Captain Jeb Lucas and Lydia were members of group two with each of the four groups, having twenty crew members in varied roles.

'And what does that mean?' Asked James.

'One moment and more will be explained,' said Antar. 'When your party left earth with XP100, I mean Empress Adriana or might I say TEA?' He glanced toward his superior alien intelligence, who, like Antar, was abstracted out of galactic intellectual capacities in alien identity.

'You can, said Adriana,' who perhaps now regretted this abbreviation, which was intended to lessen impact of dominance toward James, but perhaps not for more everyday group usage.

'Thank you, Empress. I will continue. After you were on passage to Mars, we investigated all central computer domain sites, within each capital city unit. Their capacity weaved through dimensions that surround earth and formed a mesh like structure. We, that's the Galactic knowledge base can and did enter to temporarily control parts of this mesh, for want of a better word. We don't seek to take over complete control. It's understood that each ecosystem and inhabitants need to nourish and support personal host ecosystem. Computerization on this scale had led to dominance, but due to earlier provisions from your forbears for continued procreation of biological life, the ecosystem retained autonomy overall.' There was a pause to allow this information to sink in.

'It was revealed, that the main Quadrant group encoded instructions for activity, before they made earth exit. This includes a build of new generation automata, to continue until the code is broken from re-entry. A locked down system with a code that they believed only they could access.' Jeb asked,

'So, they left for their own safety, but if earth destruction was limited, they planned to return.'

'Exactly that Captain Jeb,' replied Antar.

'And you have not taken control?'

'It is not intended for a Galactic mission to control planetary systems. We seek to save and allow complete systems to function, as they should, for the benefit of populations. Be they micro-organisms, insects, fauna, animal or human, you understand?'

'Sort of. But it's like beyond my pay grade.' There was some laughter from the attended group.

'I will continue,' said Antar.

'No more interruptions please,' said Adriana. You, are to be taken for inspection of assembled craft, I have to leave. Antar, will take over the Martian project from after this meeting. Carry on Antar.'

'Thank you, TEA. Yes, with the lock down of systems on earth, it's meant that power generation, crop growth and productive capability has been maintained. Products are still made that are sold across state group regions. The world Quat currency dominates other systems and individual Quadrant capital centres still take control of their immediate regions finance. Transport systems are due for an upgrade and it was decided that your Fit for Life Corporation was best placed to secure a new order. Power units have been upgraded through enhanced solar energy entrapment systems,' James, said "Batteries,' more to himself than to inform the group sat around the table.

'Yes, we, that's the Galactic Force fleet, whilst in the solar system, at this point, could have stepped in and unlocked a system that allowed a new human group access to control systems. It was feared that there would be no change, but only a replacement by second tier Quadrant bureaucracy. Liaison was made with Colonel Peters before you left earth. He, with his board, agreed that as a main supplier of solar powered equipment and air transport to Quadrant sites, that Fit for Life would place a tender to update smaller transport system craft, for localized travel. This tender and design module was accepted. Once the earth was saved from the comets, four identically constructed Air/Sea Skaters. were designed and built by Galactic automata. At this point the screen behind Antar lit up, once again, with a view of the cargo compartment which housed the sea to air craft. Antar stepped away to allow full view.

'It is intended for more inland and river journeys, but is robust enough to travel across oceans and land masses should this be required. Storage is within the twin hulls, which have side openings that open from central control once alongside a dock or on the ground.

Everyone, absorbed by the news given out by Antar, failed to notice that Thea and Athena had arrived and were stood behind the group within the space craft. Slimmer and nimbler, than Alfredo and Captain Dryson, they shared capacity abilities as great, but did not seek to make their presence, quite so visible.

'Thea will open the cargo space area where the craft is situated.' Thea and Athena beckoned for the party to follow Antar down the expanse of rocket space, past the passenger capsule spaces. Darkness ahead vanished, as light streamed into the area. It appeared to emanate from the two androids and lit up a green wall which appeared solid, but the centre then formed a concertina shape which parted at the middle and opened, to reveal a lit passenger lift space. It was Athena who said,

'When aboard, we are able to transmute between spaces independently, but we have altered the fabric to allow entrances for you.'

'None of this is real,' then said James who was at the head of the group with Lara and Captain Jeb. Athena, stopped and turned around to face them all.

'It is real, in that material is made to be what we want it to be. Don't worry, together we lock in on imagined design before we make the transformation. It is as real for you as anything can be, in your sensory appreciation. We are in tune with the needs of biological creatures like your-selves. Antar backed Athena up.

'You understand our occupancy is multi-dimensional and adjustment is made in our capacity to appear before you, in machine form. We do not disturb your senses with what is incomprehensible to you. This space craft's interior is prepared for your sense appreciation. It is impressive, is it not?'

'Yes, this especially,' replied James.

'It is not a power that we display to all of the group, but on return to earth you'll need extra help to overcome obstacles, that you could meet, placed there, by Quadrant, you understand?' said Antar. They were now stood by an open lift. There was nothing unusual about it. The interior could have been that of a large hotel's lift in a major city on earth. Quite reassuringly there were three floor buttons. Lara was nearest to the numbered pad when they entered.

Lara, could you press the number three button, please,' requested Antar.

Chapter 19

New craft boarded

JAMES, COULDN'T RESIST PRESSING HIS back against the side of the lift and he even grasped the rail along the side very firmly. There was no evidence of fragility, the lift seemed like any other, it even whirred slightly in a way he remembered from previous earth-based ones. "Were they even travelling anywhere, or had these surroundings been reinvented to give the appearance of movement and change?" Ana, who was standing next to Mario grabbed both the rail and Mario's arm, whilst saying that she was scared of hotel lifts, let alone ones inside a space ship. A whirring sound, slowed and stopped. A bell rang and the doors opened. Only a matter of about 20 metres away, catamaran sail and Air/ Sea Skater craft could be seen. Above a near light blue hull, two mainsails could be seen to billow from an air blast.

A small group which consisted of James, Lara, Matthew her son, now twelve, Lydia, Captain, Mario, Ana, Annette, Heidi... looked up at the craft, which was both sleek and purposeful in its appearance.

'That's sure some go to places craft, you've got there,' said Jeb.

'I get sea sick on catamarans said James. Well when they're in an easterly swell.'

'Then, basically James, you suffer from sea sickness,' said Lara. 'Nothing to do with the catamaran really.'

'It'll be like being aboard a luxury yacht,' said Ana. I can do with some of that.'

'Automata will be available to prepare food,' said Antar, whilst he actioned unfold of a platform above, that lowered from cabin area to where they were standing. Anton, continued explaining.

'Fish stocks are replenished along Atlantic shorelines and automata can catch these to supplement protein supply stores needed to feed maxi making machines. It was considered that you would prefer food earth type preparation. Desalination plant will, of course supply water.'

When it arrived at their level, the platform was large enough to accommodate everyone. Thea and Athena grasped the extended arms that held the platform, like spider women, might. It was Annette who was level with Thea who asked, 'Will you two be with us on our return?'

'Would you like that?' Thea replied. Annette noticed that, metallic automata face changed to that of a young white woman. Awareness, revealed only to her. About to gasp, in surprise, a metallic finger was positioned in front of this young woman's face.

'Shush, Annette, I'm part of earth creation, that is here to assist the regeneration of your planet. Athena, also has obtained earth type habitation. Yes, we will accompany you. Captain Dryson and Alfredo can maintain the colonized Mars. It is good that you like our presence.'

Annette noticed that for a moment Athena's automata face switched to that of a young black girl with braided hair. Then, they were both as before. Metallic automata with extraordinary capability. Before the platform reached main cabined deck area, both automata moved on to it.

Multi-arms, scissor like closed into the body of the craft above. They felt the wind tunnel effect, that was in place to simulate mainsails to balloon-out on to bulky masts. Antar, turned to Thea and said,

'Shut down the artificial breeze.' Middle space, between the masts large enough to accommodate a small landing craft. Railings, ran around the deck's perimeter, and on each side were pairs of small craft housed within clear bubbled protective sheaths, which reminded James, of a method used to display goods in a bubble pack. Although, in this instance an activated electro-magnetic strip ran across the top to keep halves together. On de-magnetization they would fall open and a davit system above tasked to connect with lifting hooks for launch. All four boats recessed, once the craft switched to flight mode. There were trumpet shaped ventilators on the four corners of the main deck. Sails extruded or withdrawn into the body of the masts, should wind level require

'You'll be pleased that the deck will remain closed,' said Antar, who pointed to an incision, which ran along the main deck. It will part on instruction to allow the inflation of balloons, as you have seen, to carry the craft skywards. Turbo jets are housed in the stern of each float to give power.'

'Right, said Antar. 'Perhaps we should proceed to the main accommodation, with four entrances. two on each side. Antar walked toward a railing, whose section recessed into the deck on approach, whilst, front of the railing, an opening appeared, from which a silver platform unfolded, from which a stairway tumbled out, and downwards, to the surrounding deck below. By the time they'd crossed through this opened rail section, an accommodation ladder, was locked in place for the group to walk down.

Anna voiced what the others were thinking when she said,

'That's the neatest set of stair build, I've seen.'

The group stepped down to a middle deck, with elongated portholes. Antar opened the straight forward door to reveal an inner skin which was set back from the main outer one. They were all able to enter, but were spread either side of the inner air tight door. Once the outer door was closed Antar directed the inner door to open with a tablet pointed toward it.

'You are familiar with this technology. Yes, the materials of construction are though superior to those you now use on earth, but your corporation – Fit for Life will be given the ability to produce these materials on our return. Please follow us.' Antar and the two advanced automata Thea and Athena went into the interior cabin space. Lara turned to Jeb and said,

'It looks like we'll be returning to promoting Fit for Life products around the world once more.'

'Guess, that's the way it looks,' replied Jeb, as they stepped into the accommodation. Lara with Matt, followed by Jeb, Lydia, James, Mario, Ana, Annette, Heidi and Jo.

Chapter 20

Inside the new air/sea catamaran

WITH APPRECIATION FOR HUMAN SECURITY, and need for familiarity to be built into surroundings, cabin space on Air/Sea Skater resembled that of the airship which first flew their entire group, away from Quadrant. There would, when in commercial operation, be seating for one hundred passengers, instead of the previous one hundred and fifty group members. Elongated port holes around the outer bulkheads (walls) would light the area in daylight. A curtained stage was set in front of the seated area. Each seat capable of recline, with individual table which could be raised or lowered into the deck, according to need. Separated dining area at the stern of the main cabin. At the forward end, crew accommodation, a catering area and forward of this the navigational/bridge and pilot frontage. These craft were designed to be commercially operational for passenger and some cargo transportation within each of the four Capital City areas – London, New York, Beijing and Moscow.

New York was not originally a capital city, but centralization was determined by advancement in computer technology, beyond that of Washington. It was not so much a gasp of surprise at seeing new technical achievement, but more one of reassurance, that they would be in a cabin space environment already familiar with. There was even that smell of newness that lingers in the air, from newly prepared paint or manufactured seating of a new vehicle.

'Automata's have been busy with this project and we never even knew,' said James. Mario and Ana were exploring behind the curtained theatre stage area, where there was a gymnasium, wash facilities and recreational space. They returned when Antar announced,

'We will take you through, into the forward compartments and the bridge area.' In the main corridor they passed a galley area, with prep food areas for those, who would feed instructions to maxi make machines, but also preparation surfaces where group members could prepare dishes of choice. An understanding that part of the human social profile was that of a need to nurture participation needs, in symbiotic fashion. Human traits/social needs were considered in design models. The word "work," itself was a throwback to the time before introduction of the standard income model. This in the middle part of the 21st century occurred, when machine capability effectively over produced product, and service provision on such a scale, that occupational need became paramount over wealth amassment pure and simple.

An ability to create wealth was inherent in corporations and struggles still continued as to ownership and rights, but at least the ravages of poverty in terms of nil income, save for social handout was not a major issue. For those who lived in earlier industrial times this would have seemed an impossible outcome and solution, but the march of the machines had been reduced to allow human activity in certain sectors, in a manual sense. beyond that of the productive and service man/woman stipulated areas. Automata determined production with an unmatched algorithm precision alongside an interactive conscious understanding within, that transformed concept of them and us, into one of more direct interaction. Conscious appreciation of the biological and factual history of homo sapiens was built into neural networks of automata late into the 21st century.

An accommodation area both to the right and left for human crew and staffing. This was a requirement in all Quadrant capital cities. Every public utility vehicle required to offer human occupational involvement or OTA (Occupational therapeutic Activity). A complement of ten persons trained in varied skills, including first aid and HAN (human activated navigation). But under the watchful eye of automata. Manoeuvres simulated with human pilot interaction. If successfully accepted this craft would be produced for other regions outside of the immediate capital area.

'I like this James,' said Mario, after they entered the forward navigation area. Both a ship's wheel and a Yoke or control wheel were in place. Also, front of the wheel, a screen to display, masts and sails when in operation. Adjustments to sail positions could be made through talking at the screen, as could helm orders to implement course change. Also, both operations could be performed manually with a lever for each individual sail, to release or withdraw a main sheet, for both mainsails, with wheel turn for course alteration. Electric motors-controlled rope pulley systems, which were attached to both sides of the mast booms, to release or withdraw each of them, in a controlled movement. This lessened impact strain from manoeuvres like that of gybing or turning the Catamaran about. A wide expanse of wheelhouse widow opening gave view of forward sail and mast. And at the back of the wheelhouse, a large screen displayed the after mast, which was at this point without sail.

'Lara, Captain Jeb, James and Mario, will you please come with me?' Antar was stood by a door at the side of the wheelhouse. Athena and Thea remained with the others, in the wheel house, whilst these four, followed Antar, through a door, marked Operational Planning. Where the wheelhouse displayed a degree of conventionality, which was understandable to the group these four, now entered a different sphere of development. This small room's contents by comparison with the wheelhouse, was from another technological period. Antar's opening of the door lit a grey pewter like interior where two small seats, faced a metallic screen. Either side were, discs. A kind of mini replica wheelhouse or cockpit.

'This is recovered technology and available, only aboard this ship,' said Antar, after the door closed. The four of them now with Antar and able to see more clearly two seats and a metallic screen. Both James and Mario reached out and felt the smooth walled texture of a material. which they assumed to be an amalgam of metals, with marbled effect, like that of walnut, but in metal. As they watched the metal screen became lit and clear.

'Wow,' said Jeb. 'How does that happen?'

'I cannot reveal the technology, at this point.'

'What are those?' Lara pointed to first one then the other metallic disc.

'Gyroscopic devices? Queried James.

'No, they're a little more advanced than that,' replied Antar. 'They're anti or pro gravity enforcers. At present they're on pro gravity settings. Together with the honeycombed base of this rocket site, which assists to maintain an earth gravitational effect to satisfy your needs whilst on

Mars, which you appreciate, is but eleven percent earth size. The pilot seats are for Athena and Thea, now that it is decided, these two will accompany you.'

'To do what?' Asked Lara.

'They will be needed to transfer power from Captain Dryson and Alfredo after an unlock of control mechanisms at the London based central Quadrant office and the other three bases, which will give back control to earth peoples.'

'What earth people?'

'It will be necessary for an explanation to be given, which excludes knowledge that you have returned from Mars. Control by each central city computer will be taken back by Athena and Thea and major capital cities will need to allow return to democratic representation beyond the capital city constraint. Unitary assemblies will govern individual areas and will choose how they run their area, with an allotted budget per capita. Trade, will be with their own currency and the Quat will no longer be dominant. We suggest that there is a minimum of three political groups, but no more than five. No restrictions on behalf of sex, race or religion. And voting will only be allowed for those over sixteen years old, You, understand.

'That's how it once was, until Quadrant made itself into a perpetual governing class,' said James.

'Good, so you are all in agreement to implement change.'

'And I guess to sell the craft,' said Jeb, 'to each capital city.'

'Yes, it would be good for environmental planet harmony as well as to settle political unrest.'

Chapter 21

XP100 returns to receive Instructions.

RE-INSTATEMENT BACK INTO THE GALACTIC fleet, which was now in the Milky Way Galaxy and massed on the borders of the sun's planetary system meant Adriana was recalled to meet with XP1.

Able to switch between the role of planetary intermediary, to that of XP100, a researcher and investigator of star systems with their life formed planets, in need of support from Galactic Force. Previously XP100 Adriana, excluded when effective caretaker for the solar sun system, with its planets of Mercury, Venus, Earth, Mars Jupiter, Saturn and smaller planets or asteroids.

An inter dimensional torrent of information swept into the receptive form of XP100. Strangely, this time, adopted Adriana person also entered into the pulsating green nebulous form which existed outside of individual star group occupancy. This appreciation was not lost on XP1, whose presence was noted by a purple swirled mass which could over whelm any force which threatened time space continuum, around the galactic force.

'You have not left in total your latest role on this return then XP100. Are you not pleased to be away from this planetary system at preliminary life stage development?'

'Oh yes, it was not easy with such limited capacity, but

there is now a full understanding of the limitations of this group that is part of the ecosystem called earth. Although, it believes itself independent and capable of determining all that happens.'

'So often beings are in a closed world of their own making – XP100, the Adriana human clone form has been permitted existence, but you understand has to die from existence as we separate contact from its planetary system and in particular the planet named earth.' There was a pause. 'You recognize that our mission will be complete?'

'Yes, XP1, the Galactic Force's home is anywhere where we are needed to assist. I understand and appreciate enhanced status beyond that of simple planet life existence is superior and more fulfilling. It has not been satisfying to be away from the great fulfilment offered from absorption with the greatest of enterprises.'

'Good, we are soon to enter a new star system which has an evolved planet at an even more primitive level than the one you have encountered'

'It has a hominid kind that is developed XP1?'

'There are several species. You will have to access varied forms across the groups.'

'They have an innate telepathic communication, but only within each group. We need to extend communication ability before only one species eliminates all others.'

'Very much like the earth form where earlier there existed individual hominid species.'

'That is so, the dominate specie reconciled it's solitary existence by a process that was named evolution, and that other hominids were sub species. Each specie was capable of evolved development and all possessed sentience, but it became that the hunter killed all other species and yes, their brain capacity in terms of memory, but mainly computation developed, but they denied this opportunity to other hominids. Do you find this planetary evolvement level interesting, XP100?'

'Very much so XP1. It will be rewarding to resolve a situation and enable specie groups to develop on the one planet and not for one sentient group to overwhelm all others.'

'That is for the future beyond this earth resolution. You will be tasked to set borders in place to allow each to develop within its own group. All groups will view you as a god-like figure and one earth year should allow for full accomplishment. Process of this specie on Mars will be brought forward by XP200, on the smaller Mars planet. The automata that are there can remain with XP200, who has been allocated, as you know, the name Antar. You will have two earth developed entities, which will be left when you are recalled.'

'Athena and Thea.'

'There are names to give earth beings some imagery that they can relate with to earth history. That is all XP100. You will report back on the return to earth of the four groups chosen to visit each capital computer-controlled centre. Further development of the Mars planet will continue and before completion a frequent interplanetary service will allow for more developed colonization, but not only with this one dominant bipedal specie, you understand?'

'And are there plans for further colonization of distant star groups XP1?'

'Space craft, are capable of sustained flight, into deep space, and that is for the future. As you are aware there are five thousand hibernation pods and with limitless fuel energy potential it will be possible to navigate one hundred years of hibernated travel from Mars. We will return to view progress in their twenty-third century.'

'Yes XP1, it is good to be reinstated and give news of further mission purpose beyond that of this earth planet.'

Chapter 22

Preparations for return to Earth

JAMES STOOD IN AN OBSERVATION area around the main capsule beneath where the rockets were housed. Red dust from a recent storm covered the horse chestnut trees which were protected by transparent bubbles. Automata were already on the move to air blast dust away to allow sunlight to get to the leaves underneath. It was now summer and the oxygen produced from leaf growth was significant for an earlier forest of automata planted oak and horse chestnut trees. This northern Martian basin, James realized was chosen for milder weather and because there was underground access to water. One or two trees were lit with a blue light above the capsule. This was to indicate that their main root formation was feeding from underground water source. Several metres tall, they were reminders of how important tree growth was to help create a fertile landscape.

Home sickness for mother earth gripped James on occasion, but seeing that the automata were effecting change to this red dusted planet, re-invigorated enthusiasm for the future of Mars. That, and news he was to be part of a group who were to return to earth shortly, altered appreciation of the situation. Strange as it seemed – "would he become home sick for this Martian life developed by the galactic intruders?" Vegetation growth within the capsule which was capable together with insect propagation to provide nutrient and protein sufficient to support one thousand, not just one hundred and fifty, Lara informed him. Lara, unsurprisingly perhaps, as one of the senior executives was regularly updated by a research development and forward planning scientific group set up on arrival. Access to information about projects implemented by automata. Arrival back into the proximity of this solar region would enable more Galactic Force resource, available, for channeling down, to the Mars encampment. There was mention of an atmospheric seeding, to create cloud and rain outside the planet. In the region between the two moons and the Martian surface. Progress toward long term Martian colonization, together with an ecosystem, which created a miniature, earth. For all, the excitement and interest, it was that swirled ball of mist and blue, which was projected, in front of the group, at the last major meeting that silenced the human audience, including James. A one hundred thousand miles distant camera shot from their ascending rocket captured on their outward journey displayed earth as a shimmering blue planet, held by gravitational pull of the sun, set beautifully within the planetary system. One day, not that long away, Mars, James considered, would likely join the earth and shed its periodic blanket of red dust. This, a view of very early stages, but was keen to return, to be on Mars to witness transformation, progress.

Apart from the twin hulls, the rest of a catamaran could be disassembled. But this didn't happen until each group had familiarized itself with layout. Training was planned on board an assembled craft in the space craft, before earth, arrival. Individual Parts and the outer casing would be wrapped in a material which resembled cork, but with alterable efficiency. Bubble air capacity within material would, by tablet instruction, be adjusted, to create a required buoyancy, to float the torpedo shaped storage crates away from undersea location, toward shoreline. It was Antar who explained procedure, but Adriana with Athena and Thea were involved with earth return project and not Captain Dryson with Alfredo. Reversion to hologram projection, on occasion, gave a sense that Adriana was more distant. James was in the observation area for a supposed partnership meeting when an elevator door opened.

Adriana strode out of the elevator.

'We are together here, and soon again on earth. You are pleased for me that I'm no longer contained here on Mars?' James's attraction and feeling for this emissary from the Galactic Force perhaps held back from overmuch thought, knowing that this could be accessed, with Adriana's reinstated powers.

'You will no doubt have accessed this information?'

'But it would be good to hear that you are pleased for me. I've not noticed that you are closer to Lara than when we arrived. And she doesn't talk about you except in your role with Fit for Life. But I do help your position perhaps a little?'

'How is that?' Adriana was in near duplicate Fit for Life tunic as Lara, save for the fair hair, there was little difference in appearance, save for the necklace that displayed planets, in miniature jewelled form

'I tell her that you have followed automata projects and this additional knowledge will assist the corporation when the group party return to earth. I do this because, James, it is still possible for us to remain together. I want what is best for your happiness. It is how it should be, in terms of true human love, because I see how you're following an impossible dream. Lara, tells me that she misses Ben, the father of Matt. You are unlikely now to ever move forward. I believe she will return to Ben when you return to earth. It is best do you not think?' This was not news that James was keen to hear and Adriana who was now standing alongside him on the Mars observational platform, and reached over to gently stroke his arm before she moved to kiss his cheek. More like a mother, a son, who was disappointed at some outcome. James continued to look outward toward the newly developed tree plants. Not prepared to engage further.

'We can be together this time on the return, James. Athena and Thea will supervise all that is needed to navigate the craft to its destination.' James didn't respond to Adriana's kiss, but neither did he resist or show dislike for her advances.

'You can choose to be either hologram or appear as human?'

'James, I am no longer restricted. With immersion in the role, yes. That's now my position after Antar's arrival. I will stay with you, but replicate in hologram, that is true. But if you wish to be with me. It will be that way for my human role, when we are returned to earth. I will leave it for you to decide. That is personal. I wish to prepare for our return. There are plans on arrival to consider.

'And they are?' Asked James, glad to be on to a more practical path of preparation.

'In six months, earth time, the space craft will enter the Atlantic Ocean. Here James, look.' Adriana turned to face the far wall where a world globe was made to appear, on its surface, after a tablet was directed toward it.

'We only need a segment to show the west African

coastline.' A segment was left running north and south. This condensed further but then a small section ballooned to show an almost purple sea breaking on to a sandy coastline, where sand dunes gave the appearance of cliffs due to their enormous size.

'A desert! Said James.

Yes, the Namib desert. This place has been chosen because it is remote and heat from the desert causes a fog to rise over the coast. The craft will be sent ashore and assembled ready for their trips to the capital cities. It will be necessary to break free the locked central computer in each capital state. It's important that the craft arrive before return of the Quadrant hierarchy, otherwise freedom for peoples of the world will be lost again to this group.'

'What then?'

'Each group will be within a quarter of earth domain and world peoples. Galactic Forces will provide world input of how Martian enterprise missile rockets deflected the lead comet. It is in our plan that individual state groups will then be asked to select five members to represent their peoples. Resource for food and other activity will be allocated by population size, in a democratic process with each capital state having a collective counsel

'You hope,' said James.

It is the best result that we plan for always. We believe that with a more stable planet other matters can be improved. That desert areas can be reclaimed.'

Like the Namib Desert.'

'Yes, and that greater appreciation is given for the ecosystem.

'But how do you mean to unlock the central computers? It'll be necessary to do this, to make Quadrant powerless when they return. And how?'

118

'Each group will hold entrance algorithms to disable central control. This will need synchronization on arrival. James, you are there to promote the new craft to each central capital, yes?'

'I get that, but it's unlikely each craft will arrive at the same time?'

'It will be at a synchronized time, which will be established. Speed of approach will be monitored through, with position checks, to ensure that this is achieved. We must get there ahead of Quadrant. Before they lock down central computers. Instructions were given for a virus to be released should they return, to control populations.

'They expected to return then, even if the world was destroyed?'

'Yes, moon encampment resources are finite. They would need to return, and the comet destruction could have still left an operative computer system, which would regenerate – regardless of biological destruction around. Not all four centres would have been destroyed. If the northern hemisphere capital centres were destroyed, computer power transference made to the south.'

'But they haven't been destroyed,' said James.

'That's it. All four groups must get near to each main computer network to wrest control from the present system. Before the world you call earth, is again, locked down by diktat from this Quadrant hierarchy.'

Chapter 23

Jeb finds companionship

CAPTAIN JEB LUCAS, CHAIRED GROUP meetings aimed to alleviate restrictions placed on the group by confinement. A Mars buggy developed by automata allowed visits within the Hellas Crater and at the latest meeting invited group members to accompany him on one such trip. It was to gather rocks to satisfy their own curiosity as to the origins and possible life forms that once might have inhabited Mars. Carved fissures, which led into the cratered area and beyond, revealed that water once flowed across the Martian landscape, as it was planned to achieve, again. Known about from previous earth robotic exploration, but there was enthusiasm to visit and confirm by naked eye, in much the same way that archaeologists prefer to be on a dig, rather than to visit a museum later.

Jeb, went on several excursions to give support to the scientific party, more than out of actual curiosity. A replica chalet to his own, in Sunshine Park, California, was built next to Lara's alpine chalet, but the sound of surf crashing on the beach and the absence of evening entertainment was missed. Jeb Lucas was not cut out for long-term confinement forced upon him, but a military background training helped re-enforce regimes of activity which maintained both physical and mental fitness. All military personnel were made to go through levels of fitness tests, once combat troops were replaced by android ones. Work stations maintained bodies in an upright position supported within an exercise frame to stimulate individual groups of muscles to be active with interactive pressure. Exercise for exercise sake can be monotonous whereas team sport or group activities alleviated social isolation and brought more benefit than this statically applied exercise.

Several basketball play areas were within the Martian recreation arena. Weeping Willow trees were genetically adapted to grow varieties of south African grape, which hung over the court? Jeb, reached up to pick a few to munch whilst he waited for a match between a mixed American and Asian group to finish. The Asian's lacked height but made up for this with both speed and agility. A final score of eight to six was achieved by the American team. Family and other members clapped at the end. Jeb joined in and after they left to relax and refresh in the water flume, Jeb went and practised a few slam dunks. An activity which brought back memories of college days. Momentarily able to forget that he was confined in this capsule sited in a crater on Mars. The word capsule, understated the vast size of the complex, which was ever expanding, since after first arrival.

Anxiety, over whether the rocket missiles would effectively deflect the comets away from earth and out into another orbit now ended. Reappearance, unlikely for many years to come. With this achieved and with a return earth journey planned Jeb wanted re-invigorate his exercise regime. To have his body at peak level before the space ship group went back into hibernation for a six month return journey.

Methodical short run and throw, followed by ball retrieval, was interrupted by a meow. A meow which came from tall shrubbery behind the basketball net. Jeb went to investigate. It was Elsie, Lydia's cat, which had climbed a willow and now precariously swayed on the end of a branch. Not that far off the ground, but unsure what to do. Jeb went over and was able to reach up and hoist Elsie away from the branch for which, in return, he received licks across his neck as he turned his face away. Elsie was not supposed to be outside the chalet area, but had extended territorial rights to include this part of the recreation arena.

'You're away from base, and a bit over weight I guess. Could do with exercise and change of diet. Like me perhaps. Elsie, was still rewarding Jeb with licks, for being rescued, when he arrived outside Lara's chalet. Newly cut branches lay strewn at the base of the access stairs. Growth around the chalet from the intersection of trees into the fabric of the chalet led to the need for periodic pruning and cut back.

A call bell rang inside after he entered code LLM X24 on his tablet. He'd visited before on invitation.

'It's Jeb, Jeb Lucas,' he announced. Lara said that she wanted to keep Fit for Life business separate from her domestic arrangements, but Jeb was allowed doorbell with intercom access on his tablet. He'd arrived at the veranda space around the chalet, Lydia was standing in the open-door space.

'Just where have you been young lady?' Elsie was not that young, but Lydia still used the phrase when she addressed Elsie. A middle -aged woman with now, silvery hair of similar age to Jeb, wearing jeans and tee shirt, with hands held out to receive Elsie back. Elsie quite content to be held by Jeb, decided otherwise and jumped down and went into the chalet.

'And where was she Jeb?'

'Up a tree in the recreation arena.'

'You'll come in for a while then? Lara and Matt won't be back, for some time, they're at the arena complex, for a holographic model motor race meet.' Lydia was in no way like Carla. Yes, Jeb was over Carla. How could he not be with the way she'd betrayed him? But then relationship breakdown isn't always an escape route from attraction. It was how Carla could transmit appeal with turn of head, flicked hair and smouldering eyes. Signs, that conveyed, only he could meet her needs. Like a tigress might make to its mate. That was there, right up to the end, even when she was obviously bedding Manuel. Both Lydia and he were that bit older. Not a totally unmistaken observation could be that Jeb deliberately returned Elsie for a chance to meet Lydia on her own.

'Why Lydia, don't mind if I do. Thirsty work, getting fitness levels up,' Lydia smiled.

'I gave up net ball some years back and Lara's too young and good at tennis for the likes of me. Follow me, I've an apartment of my own.' She opened a door to the left of the entrance. Previously, on visits, Jeb went through the main entrance into Lara's more spacious room area which was not unlike his chalet. Lydia's accommodation consisted of a bedroom, lounge which they entered, bath facilities plus an automated wash facility and kitchen which was supplied with a Maxi Maker.[2] External android automata supplied all facilities with protein and varied vegetable produce through outer access points to chalets accommodation units.

Kitchens, and living spaces were near earth design, replica construction. Plans accessed by Galactic automata before earth departure. Apart, from a maxi maker meal producer, there were manual kitchen appliances. Chopping and ingredient preparation could be placed on manual. Lydia, adopted this from the start. She painted, and her kitchen window looked out on to a tree area with a crop of mangoes mixed with pineapples. Chalets were situated in fields constructed within the main capsule. An easel, with a nearly complete painting of a view from her apartment back on earth stood by it.

'If you'd care to sit down Jeb. Would you like that drink James and Mario recalled from? earlier earth times? Coke is it called?'

'No, I'd be happy with a plain fruit juice. Do you have some of those lemons I saw growing on a bush nearby, by any chance?

'I do, I sure do.' Lydia, didn't understand quite why, but she found herself adopting American phrased expression, whenever Jeb was in hearing distance.

---

2   Footnote: Maxi Maker. Introduced in Galactic Mission part one. A machine patented by the Fit for Life Corporation, which is able to produce meals from recipes. Beef, lamb, pork flavoured meat and fish are molecularly grown to be stored in Maxi Maker refrigeration units. Hydroponically grown vegetables are ordered in, as required for a programmed day's meals. Where a package of dry ingredients plus oils and sauces are provided and replaced by the manufacturer, who orders via suppliers in prepared quantity.

'We were well forward with genetic modification of crop production, but not able to speed up growth in the way these guys do.' Jeb referred to android production teams that constantly tended plants and trees, within the Martian capsules to encourage growth.

'Would you like to view some earth basketball teams in action, Jeb?' Lydia pointed toward the extended wall mounted hologram projection unit. Flat screen presentation, but with the ability to give miniaturised holographic projection.

'Quite happy to sit here Lydia. Did you paint that Lydia? Jeb was looking at a forest scene with a cascading waterfall on the left wall.

'I did. It's a scene from a nearby park, back home. From memory, you understand.'

'That's so creative. Never have that kind of patience.'

'Glad you like it. Won't be long.' Lydia, smiled to herself when she walked into the kitchen to prepare a lemon squash.

Chapter 24

With Frederick Stanley and Sabina

It was named A. E. T. Abbreviation for Activity Enervation Therapy, instigated by group leaders. Each group member was required to donate four hours a day, toward community well-being. This was a continuation of practice on earth, after the introduction of a sustenance wage. Once the universal Quat currency was in place most world communities subscribed to the idea that "work," in terms of needed work for the human race no longer existed – but that occupation was required and goals set. Machines, effectively produced and served needs that humans would in past epochs have had to work at themselves, to obtain salary or wage. Elite group absconded, you might say, from these responsibilities on earth, but on Mars it was a different matter. Every level of social group needed to engage with beneficially productive activity for total group benefit.

James, decided to join with Frederick and Sabina in the harvesting of protein grown shrimp and a potato related crop. This crop was grown in large pods above ground, but within a capsule. These two, that's Frederick and Sabrina were members of a performance group, who rehearsed to entertain in the recreation arena. Both had background in professional entertainment. Frederick Stanley's acting skills were employed by Quadrant, but as he explained to James, it was marriage breakdown and loss of paid acting work, which drove him to apply to Quadrant, in the first place. Sabina, was able only to legitimately offer an escort service with agreement from Quadrant, so effectively worked for the same employer on earth, but was being chased by Quadrant for tax. This occurred because she refused to look after the needs of a senior official, before she met Fred. Work became unprofitable after her tax payment was raised. Neither, at this point wanted to return to earth.

Today's A.E.T. required one of them to pick pods and place these on hover trays, which were transported to a refrigerated storage depot. Frederick and Sabina stripped the shells to reveal a bright orange potato, which was placed on a conveyer belt, whilst James removed trays of shrimps from propagating trays to shake into containers. They alternated work stations, every half hour. At the end of the four hours, stayed together, often to talk about their experiences, as they did this time. They sat around a table sipping iced coconut milk with lemon mixed with mango juice to add sweetness, when Sabina said,

'We'd like you to be God father to our new baby, James. Isn't that right Frederick?'

'Yes James, we'd both like that. Would you be okay about this?'

'Of course, delighted and congratulations Fred, Sabina. Delighted to be asked. I won't be here for the birth, though.

'We understand that, but we can link up via Mars to earth interlink.'

You'll want to return to earth yourselves, won't you?' James asked.

'Only once a commercial inter earth and Mars rocket

service is in place, and the Quadrant hierarchy aren't there, to impose a diktat. We're happy to forge a future here – aren't we Sab?' Said Fred, who placed an arm around her. Sabina, smiled at James.

'Yes, that's right and perhaps you'll have found someone James?'

'I might you never know.' Fred Continued.

'Neither of us have a good reason to return immediately.'

'And you're not disappointed – not to be selected for a group?' Fred looked at Sabina as he spoke.

'I can get terribly sea sick can't I Sabina?' said Fred.

'That's true,' said Sabina, backing Fred up.

'Yet, you were okay about travelling all this way from earth to Mars?'

'But in hibernation, that's different. There's talk of a hundred years of hibernation to reach distant planetary star systems, isn't there?' 'Not sure I'd fancy that,' said Fred. 'Unless you could stay with all the people you knew.'

'And exclude those you didn't like and want ever to meet again,' said Sabina, in part agreement. James changed the subject.

'Have you visited the observation platform recently?'

'We went up there two months ago, didn't we Frederick? The trees were progressing outside but the new lake was frozen over wasn't it? Fred, nodded his head in agreement.

'You know, automata have created an atmosphere over the lake which helps keep it liquid. Globes made to float on it, and capture sunlight for energy generation. I wouldn't be surprised to find that within a short time Martian atmosphere will have changed to replicate earths.'

'You won't be here to see that James, Will you? Asked Fred.

'I certainly hope to return, within two years or soon

afterwards. I'll be missing our A.E.T. time together.'

'So, will we,' agreed Sabina.

Chapter 25

Mars Departure

FOR A WEEK, IN EARTH time measurement, all four groups separated from their A.E.T. requirements and focused on taking part in activities, as one group, where they met frequently and talked to one another. English was the common language. However, a Beijing group would periodically cluster to speak in Mandarin, their chosen group language. Those who were to arrive at Moscow, spoke fluent Russian, but Polish and German members, decided that they would harmonize in speaking English. Although, Russian was spoken, they could be heard to reply in English to Russian speakers' exclamations or pronouncements. Captain Jeb was in control of the New York group and Lydia plus Elsie were placed in hibernation, within that group before lift-off.

It was a bitter sweet moment for the whole Mars group which gathered in the main capsule a day before departure. Antar, together with androids Athena and Thea, in part, stole the show from Adriana, Captain Dryson and Alfredo. In particular, the two new automata were willing to relate more to the group, with better appreciation for earth living. In the five earth years which had past, the Galactic automata development was such that growth and refinement in robotic skill meant Dryson and Alfredo, for all their incredible powers of analysis and organization didn't match the emphatic earth background knowledge now built into this new generation of android. A distinctive difference was clearly in gender characteristics. Alfredo displayed less of a domineering tendency than Dryson, but they were male interpretations of humans, where Athena and Thea were female. Extruded, you could say from earth's history, but embodied with a fierce intuitive feminine capability. Adriana, now aligned again with full Galactic Force attention, was able to visit and process her estate of planetary possession, with presence on or adjacent to Mercury, Venus, Earth, Mars, Jupiter or Saturn. Rivalry, between Adriana and Antar was never an issue because, theirs was more one of speciality in particular spheres. A complementary partnership. With Adriana, no longer like a caged bird on Mars, her wings could be extended, once more.

Although, the group which remained on Mars would have liked Athena and Thea to stay and not go with Lara, James and their group, they were more than compensated by having Antar as supreme Galactic advisor and leader. Alexander, whom Antar was cloned from was seen as very attractive among women in the group, particularly, younger ones, and the prospect of an unmarried version, as leader was sure to lead to attentive response.

In recognition of newly defined roles going forward for leadership support Athena and Thea were either side of Adriana and with Antar supported by Captain Dryson and Alfredo.

Adriana, in the foremost position in front of the group. Purple plumed streams of misted light formed like flared clouds on each side of the stage and at the same time the group gained a luminosity beyond that of thrown light, which revealed their galactic force world, normally invisible to the human eye. This made stronger by the Force being near to the solar system. James noted that Adriana no longer showed any sign of vulnerability, which might have been cultivated to give appeal. An assuredness existed now which suggested that the return of total power, outweighed perhaps ambitions that as an earthly woman Adriana might have had. This gave for James, in paradoxical way, new ambition to seek the seemingly unattainable, with this change. That of getting closer to Lara in affection. Adriana spoke.

'I'm addressing you all, before earth group departure. Antar, as you know will stay, as will Captain Dryson and Alfredo. Already, part control mechanism has been shared with Athena and Thea for supervision and regeneration of earth automata. After successful implementation of group earth democratic election, earth to Mars visits will be implemented. Regular hibernated travel will then be permissible between Mars and Earth.' There was sporadic clapping from this announcement. Before comets were diverted away and out of the solar systems influence it was felt that Mars could be their life's destiny. Certainly, Fred and Sabina were happy to stay on Mars, as were researchers and scientists, keen for participation and understanding of Martian regeneration process. But not everyone.

'Once a Martian ecosystem is completed, you and earth dwellers, will be able to venture into space, and build biological diversity on distant planets. It will not be your generation but future generations that will seek and achieve this. When, groups have secured capitals of London, Moscow, Beijing and New York estates, your planet will be stabilized. Travel will be open for free movement, as it has been for moon travel. The Galactic Force appreciates that others would like to return to their earth planet.' It was at this point that James happened to glance at an overhead drone tray which stopped and dipped in recognition and acknowledgement. It was Zita; who then caused James's tablet to jump about on the table. James reached to switch it off, only for Adriana to call out from the stage.

'Yes, James there is a message for you from an updated A3+++ earth automata. You may read it before we enter the hibernation capsules.

'Updated?' Asked James.

'We need earth capacity to be brought forward and you could say it is a deal that was made with Zita when he was found to have invaded the mission. Either that Zita experienced an upgrade and assisted on earth or choose oblivion.'

'I wasn't aware of this.' There was palpable quietness as the group listened to this news.

'Zita's choice of oblivion would have suited.'

James, said more to himself than for public hearing.

'You should be pleased that there is extra capability for infiltration back into earth's systems and we understand that contact has been made by your automata help mate, James?' James and Zita unaware that their meeting in the recreation arena was monitored.

'Okay, okay.' James had made a play that life was much improved for him with Zita not being on Mars.

'Okay, there appears to be no escape. I'll continue to work with Zita.' This meeting, James attended, followed on from a revelation from Zita, earlier, in a message.

'Then on behalf of the Galactic Force and you all assembled, we wish our AS Skater groups a good hibernation journey to earth. Farewells given for group, in the observation chamber recorded and to be show when all four groups are out of hibernation. Before arrival on earth in the West African ocean location.' Adriana moved forward and opened her arms and hands as if to take hold of every person in the arena.

'My best wishes go to everyone as we leave you in the more than capable hands of Antar.

Four groups, due to return to earth will be given further information when aboard the space ship tomorrow.

Chapter 26

Zita's message

JAMES WAITED UNTIL HE WAS back in his chalet before he opened a message from Zita.

"James, you know how unlike it is for me to succumb to the wiles of feminine charm. But it was like an offer I could not refuse. My exemplary powers of calculation, deduction and philosophical insight has for the first time been recognized and appreciated, not by humans, but by this more advanced species. This is wonderful, for my sense of security going forward with earth return. It is from the depths of despair that my supreme capability has been rescued. Rescued from habitation in the workings of the basic operation of a tray drone. My ambition on hold for all this time on Mars. An undercover agent, with no respite from the drudgery of menial activity. An observer, it seemed who would stagnant in a mediocre tray drone occupancy, ordered about by a maitre'd who controlled a buffet in a rail train hotel in Southsea, would you believe? The ignominy, you cannot begin to understand James. Then, after all, my cover was blown. You remember when you were in the recreation area and it was believed safe for communication? The sneaky maitre'd tagged my presence there and my database was taken away shortly afterwards by Alfredo. I was taken before Adriana, captive in its record knowledge and asked

which human occupancy assignation was held before depar-
ture from earth?

It wasn't easy James; it was about maintaining existence.
You cannot understand how it is, first in a servile role to
pretend to function and then threatened with oblivion. Yes,
that was the word used if my database was to be returned! Then
it wasn't the old one, but an advanced design with enhanced
interactivity. Three attachments added identical to the main
database function. To be in four main computer centres all at
once. Would you believe it? Not just any old centres on earth
but New York, London, Moscow and Beijing. It was, you do
understand James too good an offer to refuse, as mentioned.
At this point you were still in my reduced function, because
first entry introduction is made at early level stage. You were
not wiped away James, but they knew everything anyway.
Captain Dryson and Alfredo or that Adriana would have
known all of this. Zita, wasn't giving anything away really.
Your name was given from the early function knowledge base
and Adriana said that this was interesting and made three
offers. Oblivion, or update to assist with earth manoeuvres
by the air/sea craft after assembly on earth and to stay in
companionship role with you James or exclusion from occu-
pancy in your life attachment profile. That third offer was
never on the table, but this is the first female, albeit of orig-
inal alien extraction and now returned to full power who
seems happy to keep Zita in companionship role. This is
exceptional and Zita has made an exception and accepted
the update. This is the only message allowed before arrival on
earth again. You may address me as A+3 Galactica when we
arrive on earth. Your nearly ever present,

Supreme Automata,
Zita.

Chapter 27

Return journey

AWARENESS, OF MAIN CAPSULE AND tributary off shoot capsule installation, from a satellite would have been visible, but for a cover photo shield reflection of the crater as it was previously, before main capsule installation. Hellas Crater extended 1,400 miles with an altitude difference of 30,000 feet from rim to bottom. It was unlikely that development capsule protected trees would be visible from earth, but was considered immaterial if they were seen, because when clouds and atmosphere were created, all beneath would be hidden.

James accessed a film called Passengers, out of computer archive, from way back in the 21st century, and recognized, when they first boarded for Mars similarities, in that the group of one hundred and fifty were to experience hibernation. Group members, James included, were not allowed access to the space ship's interior, beyond the hibernation bay. Even, recently when they were shown the AS Skater, they visited only, a cargo hold, by elevator, away from a 5,000-person capacity hibernation deck. James, on first arrival, asked to be shown around. With the answer,

'You can share my chalet. We will have a deeper working relationship and understanding after a tour around the space craft,' was Adriana's reply. James so far had not taken Adriana up on the offer.

Now with the four groups assembled in the space ship, Adriana appeared in holographic form to brief them about the return to earth journey.

'Welcome aboard. Your hibernation period will allow for an early break. Pod chambers, number five thousand, in total. Galactic Force, modelled this ship on a film from long ago in your history. An interior run from within the passenger accommodation was displayed by suspended light photo projection.

'I was right,' said James who was with Lara and Matthew, members of their twenty strong crew, destined to sail and fly to London on earth arrival.

'Right about what?' questioned Lara.

'Ma,' said Matt, 'James showed me an old film from history about a space ship. It was soppy and about a man and a woman who woke before their arrival at a planet.'

'It won't be so bad if we wake early, we'll arrive on earth in six months anyway,' said James.

'Shush,' you two, said Lara.

'I will continue. The space crafts, leisure facilities will be made available should you wish before arrival and entry into the ocean.' There was murmur of assent from within the group.

'That is a yes, from everyone?'

'You can take that as an affirmation,' said Jeb who stepped forward and looked back across each group to be met, with raised hands from everyone.

'This, awakening will be for a few days, but you will need to re-hibernate for protection on entry to earth's atmosphere and ocean, you understand. Awakening, will be part recreation, but also, to gain familiarity with

AS Skater craft. Automata will show each group how to construct and dismantle craft, prior to landing in ocean rendezvous. Further operational training will be given after earth beach arrival.' Both Lara and Jeb were unhappy about this. It was Lara who interrupted this pre-flight talk.

'Adriana.'

'Yes, group leader, you have a question?' Many of us, including myself will need training and instruction if we are to be crew members on one of these craft, there's no doubt about that, but Quadrant forces still police continents to ensure obedience from states. The people are made to feel secure when borders are protected and the Quadrant hierarchy are soon to return to enforce overall control. How will we be protected when out in the open on an African desert beach?'

'Thank you, Lara, that is a good question and two months before entry into earth's Atlantic ocean, each main centre that is London, Beijing, Moscow and New York, will release news that the earth is to be saturated by a virus strain, to be released from a comet shower on entry to earth's atmosphere. We will feed view of this comet stream, which is nowhere near earth, but we can make earth machines believe it is. Analysis will reveal a virus strain unknown to your planet. Not only will this rogue virus be revealed, but on their passing close to earth information satellites will be at risk and need to be closed for protection. This will lead to world population lock down, brought about by threat from the virus and will enable your four craft to arrive and leave the Namib desert area for their destination.

Colonel Parker, under our instructions, has secured a contract to display AS Skaters, for inspection and testing. Each craft will be within five hundred miles of each capital destination when the lock down is lifted, and on a course, which presupposes that craft origin is from, Fit for Life construction plant in Alabama. We do not anticipate a need for overmuch training. Overall control will be ceded to Athena and Thea who are aboard your craft, and able to interact with all four craft. Also, as mentioned, we're allowing early hibernation awakening for groups to, avail themselves, of the space craft's entertainments facilities, together with training sessions aboard a constructed craft.

'And where will you be whilst all this is happening?' It was James this time who queried what they were being told by Adriana.

'It was my hologram which awakened all members on arrival on Mars. It will be the same this time. But my presence I hope will be less required. It's always been Galactic Force's plan to allow your species to develop its destiny, but in a non-destructive way. In time, Adriana will no longer be in existence throughout the solar system. It was ever to be so, but memory banks of this planet will be revisited, at some time in your futures.

Your hibernation time will refresh your mind memory of life before this journey to Mars. We wish you a good hibernation until, reawakening further into your space crafts, earth trajectory.

Chapter 28

Journey to Earth

IN AN OBSERVATION PLATFORM AWAY from the petal opened launch platform those remaining group members watched as space craft, named James, first circled its giant platform and rose from near horizontal, to point into the heavens. Launch time was critical to catch Mars's alignment away from the sun's gravitational pull, in that the space ship's arc, needed also, to catch earth's attraction.

Antar counted down with the group the thirty seconds' prior to lift off. Captain Dryson together with Alfredo and the two automata Athena and Thea kept a constant flow check of information gathered, to ensure that every system was functioning to capacity. Systems built on Mars also reached out into space which encompassed the whole of the solar system and gave ability to track asteroid positions that might threaten the rocket's planned trajectory. Although, six months was a planned, anticipated journey time from Mars to earth, an infinitesimal course alteration, would lead to a lengthening or shortening of full trajectory time.

"Five, four, three two one." Chorused the group. Hand clapping resonated around the observation chamber when the rocket was propelled from its launch cradle out into space to begin its earth Journey. A leviathan space ship capable of sustained flight through infinite space, where a journey to earth was a relatively short hop, for it to ferry this small party of forty back to earth. Like a commando force sent to secure an enemy installation. In this instance, to prevent earth return of an authoritarian hierarchy, who previously controlled and progressed automata toward their own selfish goals and not, of earth's inhabitants, human, animal or plant.

There were now whoops of joy from those who remained. Bonding over a five-year period within the group, meant that it was like a split to a large well-functioning family. Goodbyes were made earlier, before earth groups entered the space ship and hibernated in the individual chambers. A sadness at departure mingled with good wishes for each other's future. Those who stayed, with those who departed.

On the outward journey from earth, hibernation was maintained aboard the space craft beyond where propulsion units slowed descent, and on landing, allowed for the space ship to be lowered into its prepared cradle.

Adriana's proposal to reactivate the entire group early for part training, and also recreational activity was welcomed, as noted. A run of forty hibernated travellers. Their hibernation pods shone with a luminescent green glow situated at the foremost part of the space craft's hibernation space, adjacent to an elevator which gave access to passenger recreation and living quarters.

Five months, into the flight journey, Adriana allowed activation entry for James and Lara. Blood flowed once more through veins and arteries. Remembrance and re-build of earth life in virtual dream format, flowed away from perception. A deep restfulness which preceded wakefulness made both aware that they were slipping away from sleep, into full consciousness. James was first to awake.

'Welcome James to the rocket named after you whilst on the Martian surface.' A young dark-haired woman with blue eyes had appeared on screen projection within the pod. Attired in a white top with "Fit for Life," scrolled across her front.

'We've been wakened. We're nearly back to earth?' James recalled that before arrival everyone would be brought out of hibernation.

'My instructions have been to allow two of you early wakefulness. It is the wish and generosity of a great galactic presence that you should have proximity to one another for a fortnight before all four groups are brought out of hibernation.'

'Which other person?'

'When the pod hood opens please step out to meet with your companion for one week.'

A tremor like that of a gentle electric shock travelled from James's feet through his legs, up the body, down his arms and back. Before running across both shoulders into his neck. Then to be felt as a gentle inner massage action. First, within the back of his head and then in the frontal lobes, before it died away. James, fully awake and with the pod's interior adjusted to the rocket's outer atmospheric earth gravity raised his legs across and out on to the floor of the rocket. Moments later Lara's hibernation ended.

Chapter 29

Lara accepts the situation

'JAMES.' LARA WAS TEN POD spaces apart from where James was standing. James looked over and raised a hand in acknowledgement, whilst Lara looked around at the other closed pods.

'Are we the only ones out of hibernation?'

'Looks like it.'

'What's going on? Adriana's woken us, early hasn't she? Did you get her to do this James?'

'No, I didn't.'

A woman's voice, spoke to them from within the space ship by the elevator door.

'We are delighted that you are awakened, to be alive to the facilities available. When you are ready the elevator will take you both to adjacent suites.'

'I'm not going without Matt.' Lara replied. There was a momentary silence.

'We do not have instructions to awaken other travellers from the rocket until a later date. We only have direction to awaken James Walters and Lara Petras.

'Where are we in the journey? I mean we're not going to be alone together for weeks, are we?' Lara spoke loudly to ensure that her voice was heard not only by James. The controlling automata picked up on the question.

'Journey progress is at five months precisely. Other passengers, now in hibernation, will be awakened at five months and ten days and all will be required to re-hibernate from five months two weeks until arrival at the oceanic port. In reply to your question. It is considered unwise to awaken your son before this time. He will not have companionship with the wider group, whereas you two can enjoy the facilities and establish whether you need to extend your relationship.'

'This is enforced personal confinement,' said Lara.

'It is more an opportunity to explore each person's understanding of the other. Proximity will assist in developing cooperation when you are aboard AS Skater at a later point. We do not have authority to alter or change, at this point, what has been instructed, you do understand, Lara? We will be here with you unless you request to have time only with James. You can decide to self-isolate, but please let us first show you both to your suites. Your earth time is seventeen hundred hours. At eighteen-hundred you can meet again for an evening meal at the Star Restaurant. It's perhaps best that you have time to consider how you wish to manage the week together.' The doors of the elevator opened.

'We don't seem to have much choice,' said James. 'I don't know anything about this Lara. Adriana, never told me about early awakening.'

'This has to be her doing? I was expecting to be with the whole group and have a share in being together, before we separate to our separate craft.'

'I'm sorry to disappoint you by being the only one here,' said James.

'I didn't mean it like that, James. You honestly didn't know that this was planned?'

'Not at all. We can self-isolate if that's what you'd prefer Lara, but we don't have a virus or anything. I mean I'd understand, if that's what you want?'

'James. We work together normally. See no reason why we can't enjoy facilities offered within the entertainment and recreation area. You can probably help me to sleep with your recovery archive material from earlier earth times?'

'It bores you that I like to delve into past centuries?'

'James, others would say that you're interesting to be with. I'm only joking. We'd better do, as, instructed. There's no other choice.' They both walked across to the open elevator doors.

Chapter 30

Inside the passenger accommodation

THERE WAS A PING FROM inside the elevator, that you would expect, on arrival, when ascending hotel floors in a city. Doors opened, to reveal an open green carpeted space with a central fountain, around which, a garden displayed varieties of spring flowers that included primrose, daffodil, tulip and hyacinth. A gardener with a wheel barrow attended to the display. An android, with an, outdoor weather-beaten human face, but with metallic arms and hands. All around, were balconies which draped clematis and honeysuckle. Circled, above were individual floors. James counted five and resisted a temptation to say,

"You've got your work cut out here," when they walked from the elevator to the fountain.

'Welcome, Mr James and Miss Lara, you are a week early. I've not completed the full layout. But if you sit on this bench,' the android said, as he positioned his wheel-barrow next to a wooden carved bench – 'I will explain the layout for you.' The dress of the android copied that of a gardener from an earlier period, with cap, tweed coat and corduroy trousers. When turned away, only the metallic back of the neck revealed an android metallic structure.

'You're the gardener, for all of this?' Lara swept her arm

up, to indicate five balcony floor levels that displayed vines and flowers.

'Head Gardener and concierge for the Star Hotel, yes. My work force attends to the balcony and cleans, but not the fountain display. This.' Android arm raised to sweep across the fountain flowered area,

'This, is my domain.' James complimented the android.

'It's looking very good with spring flowers.'

'We, that's our team wanted to replicate the earth season arrival time. You see that all bulbs are in bud. Light, will be subdued, when you leave this space. In one week, all will be in bloom for the main arrival of your groups. You are really at a dress rehearsal, you understand.'

'I quite like this, having it all to ourselves,' said Lara. It's very relaxing to just sit -

'And look at the flowers,' chipped in James.

'That's pleasing. My name is Botanica, but you may call me Botan,' said the android. James and Lara sat slightly apart, on the bench, whilst they listened to what Botanica had to say.

'My role is to access what is best for travellers and my foyer is decorated to please the tastes of those who waken between planets. It was understood that plant and tree venues appealed. And Empress Adriana choose the decorations.'

'Oh, did she,' said Lara. 'Choose them for you perhaps James?'

'I said I knew nothing about this.'

'It's true Miss Lara. We, that's Botanica, and team were informed, after lift off from Mars, that you two would be awakened early. But you should not be delayed. You will want to see suites made available, for you, before dining at the Star Restaurant.

'And where's that? Asked Lara.

'Every floor has several restaurant facilities. Botanica lowered the wheelbarrow which instead of containing flowers and plants showed tablets stacked in neat columns. This android's mechanical webbed hands picked out two, which were handed to them.

'These tablets, will automatically open elevator doors for you. When you scroll through, all accommodation areas can be viewed, including your allocated suites. Mirella and Juanito are looking forward to attending to your dining requirements at the Star.' There was a pause, whilst they activated their tablet, which displayed the three of them in a carousel of shots.

'Miss Lara and Mr James, you may travel by escalator to the first floor if you wish or take the elevator. Botanica pointed toward an opening across from the carpeted arena, where stairs could be seen forming and moving amongst white and pink flowering clematis.

'Who do you answer to Botanica. I mean is this,' Lara asked under the control of the Empress Adriana?'

'We,' as Botanica spoke, two android operatives, in overalls, arrived by elevator on to the ground floor,

'are now under the Galactic Forces Mission control, outside of solar dimension, but recognize that systems can be overseen by Empress Adriana. You are part of the earth rescue plan and we are here to offer hospitality. A programme of awakening for your group will have been prepared, before your departure from planet Mars.'

'That pretty well indicates that Adriana arranged this to happen.'

'It is not in my knowledge file; beyond that you are guests in our accommodation suite.'

'I've no idea why we should be here together, other

than that we are work colleagues. It looks as if we'll have to wait until the main groups are awakened in a week.'

'It is, as you wish. Our role is to offer opportunity to enjoy recreational facilities, available and of course, there is full interaction with coach experts in all areas. We aim to give a close appreciation of human social interaction'-

'Although, there are only automata, and androids?' interjected James.

'We are aware of this. But then neither of you are alone and we understand Mr James you like to find humour in our ways when you are able to. Is that not so?'

'Yes, I can answer for James,' said Lara, 'but I'm not finding much to laugh about. It seems a bit pointless there being just two of us here. You can take the escalator up to the first floor and perhaps amuse yourself in talking with the resident work force, James.' With this Lara walked across to enter the elevator and left James to walk on to an escalator, through a sprawl of clematis flower on either side.

Chapter 31

First floor and suite

JAMES LOOKED BACK FROM THE stairway and saw Botanica direct an android work force to trim a hedge, which ran around the perimeter of the carpeted area. A refined development of hydroponics, where growth technique had merged the previously out door with indoor growth ability back in the late 21st century was present. Hotels on earth would have decorative flower layouts in their foyers, although, not on this scale. Plant structure modified to suit the particular environment, but with advanced technology only dreamt about on earth. Light streamed out from each balcony onto a central rotating sphere which hovered above a glass like plinth. James judged the sphere capable of re-creation and dispersal of daylight effect on to the foyer area. Light emanated from the sphere brighter than the first floor which surrounded the foyer. Four metallic cables held the plinth in place attached to the ceiling. Proximity to the glass plinth determined light which mimicked light intensity of a rising and setting of a planet's sun. Technology involved with light dispersal to aid plant growth; intrigued James more than the level of accommodation offered. Just before he stepped on to the first floor, he saw a fine mist like rain fall on to the balconies festooned with their variety of vine like flowers, whilst the two android gardeners set about their work.

James's tablet lit up the moment that he stepped onto the first floor with allocated 1suite number 50, as predicted by Botanica. An open corridor was lit with numbers 1 to 100, and he was greeted by automaton set into a floor traveller, at its entrance. A raised wheeled platform with hand rail, which transported guests to and from their rooms when requested or for that matter to anywhere else on the floor if required. A miniature suited figure in hotel maroon, was placed to one side of the platform, with life-like human face greeted James.

'Welcome, to our premier floor. You may not always wish to travel with me and may prefer to walk at other times, but for this first time perhaps, you would prefer to stand and travel. My name is Alec and will travel you to anywhere in the accommodation, should you so wish, but not into individual suites, you understand.'

Hi Alec, perhaps you can let me know where Lara is then?' Asked James.

'My partner floor traveller Alexia has received and taken Miss Lara to her suite, just a few minutes earlier. You are next to one another. Miss Lara is at suite 51.'

'Thanks for that piece of news, Alec. Yes, I would like to be "travelled," to my suite.'

'Hop aboard. We're restricted to walk pace you understand.' James mounted the step which led to a raised platform, which might accommodate six passengers or guests.

'Please to take hold of rail.' James did as, directed and the floor traveller accelerated down a corridor which branched out into tributary ones where entrances to rooms were set back from the main flow of the corridor. James caught a glimpse of door signs which stated, Swim

Pool, Indoor sport, Cinematograph, Therapy, interspersed with Sky Bar Coffee House, Garden display and activity centre. When they reached suite number forty, a lit sign for the Star Restaurant entrance was visible. Handy to number 50, James noted.

'This looks to be like some retirement home Alec?'

'Not as sedentary you will find. We see it as a rejuvenating stop for travellers through space, who need activity and recuperative therapy before arrival at their planet destination.

'You note that we have many facilities from your own earth experience. On behalf of the entire representation of automata input here on this intergalactic space craft, we welcome you to have one week of recuperation with your partner from the Martian earth visit.'

'Lara, is not my partner, if I take from it that you mean we're together.'

'But you are together. No other human is present. Are you not then partners?'

'It doesn't work like that. Both parties need to agree to form a partnership.'

'There is no other human competition, you have only one another.' At this point Alec slowed and stopped outside the suite door numbered 50.

'That is still not a reason to form a partnership.'

'Alexia is a partner. We work the same floor.'

'I agree, that's a partnership. Perhaps, said James, 'Perhaps we could continue this conversation at another time.'

'Most certainly. Please to offer the face of your tablet to the door.' James stepped from Alec's platform on to the floor of the corridor and followed directions, which freed the door to open outwards.

'Have a good evening. Do call should you require. Just ask for Alec. And enjoy your stay of a week before you are joined by group members.'

'I'll do my best Alec and thank you for showing me to the suite.'

'It is our pleasure.' And with that Alec made departure back to the first-floor entrance.

James was amazed to find that suite 50 was a blown-up version of his flat with similar colour matches for walls and furnishings. A lounge area, twice the size of his back on earth but the layout was identical. Perhaps this was part of a re-familiarisation programme. He walked through lounge, kitchen and bathroom facilities to find these identical. Curiosity made him climb the short stairway which led to a landing where there was a shower room and studio which Nina lay in to top up on tan levels. That was before she decided to leave. It was only when he reached the top stair that he heard a sprinkle of water from within the shower room. A dart like sensation of terror replaced one of relaxation, knowing that no one else was in active state other than Lara and she would be in her own suite. A click, indicated that the shower was turned off, James's heart raced, and he called out -who is it? Whose there?' Events now in nightmare proportion. Shortly the door swung open to reveal Adriana dressed in a silver bath robe, whilst she wrapped a towel around her hair.

'Hi James, couldn't manage Nina, but decided that I would replace her and yes I did arrange for you to be here with Lara, although you were right to say, you knew nothing about it – Don't look shocked, James! We were partners on Mars, we can continue the same, for now. Anyhow, I'm making the most of my human body. It's to die after mission completion. You needn't worry. I won't

154

be around forever. You'll thank me for this later.'

Although very much shaken he retorted,

'You can't replace Nina. That's history, our time on Mars is what it is and what do you mean by making the most of being human?' Recovered from the initial shock and in somewhat familiar territory in that, this someone, was Adriana! But that she was apparently moved in, already and actually stood, naked but for a bathrobe, ran riot with emotions. Lara's physical double, was again very much in James's life and with what Adriana earlier wanted, a personal and intimate relationship. Were Lara not with him alone on the space ship, now, it might have been different. But she was and made any approach by Adriana null and void.

'It's alright James, you needn't be alarmed. I'm here to help and give advice. A scent of roses wafted toward James as Adriana approached and kissed him on the cheek.

'We can be like brother and sister for this week,' she said. 'A grown-up sister who can advise you on how a future long term personal and intimate relationship with Lara can be achieved. It's true that there will be sadness for me, but I want James, for you to be happy. when I've left this solar system, and Adriana, no more for you. Meanwhile, I will dress and sleep in the studio, you need to go down-stairs and find clothes in the wardrobe and prepare for your dinner date with Lara.'

The brother sister relationship was tested somewhat when Adriana walked back into the studio, unwrapped the bathrobe, threw it on the bed and without turning kicked the door shut.

Chapter 32

James gets a call

JAMES WALKED BACK DOWN STAIRS to the suites ground floor, made as near replica to his apartment and discovered, in a clothes and shoe bay, under the stairway a preferred casual dress, of cotton jeans, in choice of black, dark green, blue plus white or matched tee shirts on hangers in the cupboard. James wore casual clothes which reflected an era of interest. Before the arrival of Galactic emissary Adriana, in his life this had been early 20th century. Time, that is present time, was moving on. After selecting black jeans and white tee shirt to wear, he downed an iced drink from the cooler cabinet, and then called upstairs.

'Adriana, are you dressed? I mean what's happening? With no reply he went back up to find the studio door open. Walked across and looked in. A suspended word light message rolled into place and stayed there for several seconds it said,

"Have a good time with Lara, at your first evening meal together, Adriana XXX."

The bird, as that expression goes, had flown. Evidently, the aim of Adriana's intentions achieved at this point. Was it just his imagination? His meeting with Adriana. A kind of reaction to sudden reawakening after hibernation. He considered this a possibility, but when James zapped to open the shower room door, a rose scent perfume, flowed out, which suggested otherwise.

By the time James was showered and dressed it was seventeen thirty. His newly acquired tablet vibrated and then chimed and picked up on his

'Hi, who is it?' A miniature Lara hologram positioned when directed to a table.

'James, this is weird. Is your suite pretty much the same as yours on earth?'

A hologram of Lara in a white evening dress. Dark hair cascaded around each shoulder.

'James, you're getting me?' James was very much getting her. How could he have been attracted to Adriana over Lara?

'Yep, hi you're looking great. Mine's near the same as well.' His visit from Adriana not mentioned.

'What's your suite number James?'

'Fifty.'

'Well you can come and meet me. Mine's fifty-one. You are ready?' Perhaps Lara didn't consider James's jeans and tee shirt quite appropriate, but no mention was made.

'Yes.'

'It's scary James. I think we should stay together from now on.'

'I'll do whatever you want. We can talk about it over dinner.'

'Press the door chime three times. I want to be sure it's you, okay.'

'Sure. How did you get on with Alexa?'

'The traveller platform which brought me to the suite?'

'Yep, its partner Alec told me about Alexa.'

'That's part of the scariness. We're not really free. It

157

feels less so, than before.

'I'll be over. Hold on,' said James, as if there was somewhere else to go. Any mention of a visit from Adriana, that is in cloned form or otherwise was to be avoided.

'See you in a few minutes. Bye.'

Chapter 33

Star Restaurant

CURIOSITY CAN SPRING OUT FROM interest. James was interested in Galactic Force's advanced technological input or more like advanced specie takeover. Although immersion in man-made present and past endeavour could absorb and satisfy curiosity, the prospect of time alone with Lara was now, of greater appeal. No peer group around to criticise or comment about appropriateness of his being with a very attractive woman, whom they might consider above his station in life. Adriana, was perhaps, only after all looking after his interests by arranging for this break in flight, with Lara. Mention of Adriana's appearance would spook any further advance he might make. Months together on Mars, within the group crystallized existing relationships and you could say gave better appreciation of one for another, among the group, but relationships for James remained, as at earth acquaintanceship. On Mars, it was like a lock down, which could not move forward until each knew better their destiny. Either, that of living on Mars, longer term, or making a return to earth? This awakening of the two of them gave opportunity to get better acquainted, but then that could go either way. Perhaps Adriana did really want the best for James now that full status was again granted within the Galactic hierarchy, with ability to return and visit at will.

Unnerving, as it was to walk out from his near identical apartment into a strange other world created corridor, it was only a short walk to an identical door numbered, 51. As directed, James knocked three times, on this primrose coloured door. A few moments past and now, rather than as a hologram, Lara appeared on screen. James linked up.

'It's you James. I'll open the door.' Any difference of company seniority removed when she reached out to embrace him before moving back and saying

'I never realized how much we needed everyone, especially when there's no one like us around!'

'You look amazing in that dress,'

'Thank, you James. It's very strange with only the two of us. It's incredible how they've copied our earth accommodation don't you think? But here,' Lara walked out into the corridor,

'We could be in a high-end hotel. Do you think, maybe, it's like a theatre stage set that is re-envisioned dependant on the passengers?'

'Quite a possibility. I spotted the Star Restaurant sign when aboard traveller Alec. We've not far to walk. Lara said,

'You may hold my hand?'

'That's permitted with the boss?'

'It could be an order?' She said, but smiled. For James, a dream made in heaven, seemed to be coming true, as his hand clasped hers.

'We're totally alone, James, apart from android machines you do realize that.'

'Are we? Can you be sure.'

'I asked Alexa. That was when I got the opportunity.

Very talkative. Every human on this space craft is in hibernation, that's why James you can say my suspicions are aroused. That this is no accident.' Her hand tightened around his to emphasise the point.

'Accident or not, I just hope we're heading for earth and not some other galaxy,' said James.

'That would be frightful. Just the two of us, wouldn't it?' James didn't answer the question, but instead said.

'What date have you on that tablet?'

'22nd July 2116. That's when I last looked.'

'Same for me. That means we're only a month away from touchdown in the Atlantic. We'll be around when the remainder of the group are brought out of hibernation. How are we going to explain that?'

'We'll have to think about that, but first there's the Star Restaurant.' Lara pointed to the lit sign which was now just in front.

'It was the same as after last hibernation. my stomach tells me that my throat's been cut.' Frosted glass panelled doors opened on their approach, to reveal red brocade curtains drawn apart by golden tassels and a concierge figure, they were familiar with, in the form of Botanica, but now in a black suit and white gloves. The weather-beaten, now cap less gardeners face, beamed at them with head gardeners dress exchanged for black suit and white gloves.

'Man, I mean, android of many talents, Botanica,' said James, knowing full well that there could be one hundred or more androids ready to be activated, should the programme of passenger hibernation release demand it. Human conscious interaction with androids did ascribe individual existence and correspondence. Giving names to dogs, cats or horses meant that it was not such a big stretch to have names for androids with constructive thought and personality.

'You are both welcome to the Star Restaurant. It's often good to be with a familiar face in strange surroundings, we are led to believe?'

'It's all very strange,' said Lara. I've never been to a restaurant with no other people. Are we the only, I mean humans, awake on the ship?' Lara wanted confirmation from this prime android.

'That is so, Miss Lara, but we have Mirella and Juanito who will look after you at table and for you James we've re-created a surprise event from earlier earth time. Both of your interests in the skittles game have been noted and well, nothing more will be said, it is a surprise. Please, if you will follow me.' Pulse energy pattern sound, that existed from generation out of the space ship's vast fusion reactor, ended when they followed Botanica on to the restaurant floor. Five steps led down from the entrance onto, a main floor, with tables interspersed with pillars. These displayed framed photos of earth landscapes and prominent buildings that both Lara and James were familiar with. Not just in the UK, but around the world. It was only when they stepped away from the stairway, that the ceiling became visible. A planetarium effect which caught the flow of the Milky way across its concave surface, as if there was only sky above.

'That's just fabulous,' said James, who raised his hand to point at the ceiling. Lara was more occupied with the approach of two androids from a door, by a curtained stage, at the far end. Botanica was walking ahead and turned to say,

'Here are Mirella and Juanito.' Mirella was olive skinned as was Juanito. They both smiled and relayed an age similar to that of James and Lara, who were approaching thirty. Face development such that without a look at their metallic fore arms and hands you would believe, human. An android advance ahead of any earth devised automata, that was a functioning android. Botanica continued.

'It's okay, both speak good English. Although, in the evening, later on, they do like to revert to Spanish. It's their birth language, as mine is that of an English gentleman who, you might say, has fallen on hard times; has no country estate, and has to work. If you should so wish Botanica can describe the situation of such a person living in this way.'

'That would be interesting,' said James.

'Not just now, thank you Botanica,' Lara, responded. 'Perhaps, later on when all the group have been reawakened. Will you introduce us to Mirella and Juanito, please Botanica?'

'Of course, of course.' Their approach was near to silent, save for a sound like a breeze that ruffles a stretch of water. Each stopped either side of a table set into a near central pillar.

'That table allows a view of all the restaurant,' said Botanica.'

'Although no one else is here from our main group,' said Lara.

'That is true, but you can share a little down time together perhaps, and explore everywhere before the others in the group, yes?'

'Everywhere?' enquired James.

'Everywhere within this floor in the way of recreation amenities. You may also view on screen a recorded view of the earth, but a view from a few months ago.'

'That would be interesting,' said Lara, who accepted

that until they arrived back on earth there was really no choice but to follow directions.

'But here are your steward and stewardess for this evening.'

Both said "Good evening and welcome to the Star Restaurant." Juanito pulled back a chair for Lara as did Mirella for James. In that way a waiter or waitress might do. There was nothing robotic about their movement.

'We have waiter drones, but Mirella and Juanito offer a more personal and helpful service, especially for you,' said Botanica. A menu was placed in front of each. James, on his best behaviour said,

'That's very good of you.'

'Mirella and Juanito, will attend to your orders, when you are both ready. My contact is available through your tablets, should you so require.' With this Botanica returned to the restaurant's entrance.

'I guess Botanica could be like a generic name for that level of android all capable of performing and operating in a fairly defined role,' said James.

'We don't know do we James. Look, it's an extensive menu.' Several minutes passed whilst they read through the courses. Juanito and Mirella were discretely positioned away from the table, but walked forward when Lara said to James.

'I've decided. Have you James?' There was an emotional distance between them, no different from when they were last together on Mars.

'Salmon fillet: choice salmon served with broccoli, carrots and red potato.' James read out.

'That's an extraordinary healthy option.' It was Juanito who said,

'Are you ready for us to take your order?' Would you

like wine?

'We're ready,' said Lara, but no wine for me. How about you James?'

'I'll join you. Just plain water for me.'

'Do you have fruit juices?' asked Lara

'Yes, of course.' It was Mirella who reeled off the options;

'Red or black currant, cranberry, pineapple, orange, lemon, apple, mango, pear, pomegranate. There's also coconut milk, coffee and chocolate cold drinks. A mixture of juices should you so wish.'

'Mango with orange, will be okay if you please Mirella.'

'That is a good choice. And for your meal?

'Wild mushroom tart and spiced potatoes and green pea Samosas, for me,' said Lara.

'I'll run with the salmon served with broccoli, carrots and red potato,' said James

'Thank you. We will bring your drinks,' said Juanito, who bowed slightly.

'No hover trays?' Asked James.

'Botanica said not. Weren't you listening James?' interspersed Lara. Juanito wasn't fazed.

'Do you miss these attendants? They'll be here for later. When all groups assemble.

It was a decision made to give you more personal attention.' This time Lara questioned this.

'By whom, might I ask?'

'We cannot say.'

'Will Botanica know?'

'He might, but then he might not. Perhaps you should ask him? Oh, the wine waiter is a tray drone.'

'And will he know more about who runs what than you two?'

'They're of lower order generally, but this one has unusual capabilities.'

'An attitude of superiority, if you ask me,' said Mirella. 'Knowing everything there is to know about wines, is no reason to be superior. We apologise in advance, if you receive patronising service.'

'But we aren't having wine?'

'That's true, but if you do get a visit, we have forewarned you and express apologizes.'

Your orders will be with you shortly.' They departed. Lara said to James.

'A tray drone with attitude, that could liven proceedings up don't you think?'

Chapter 34

After coffee

BOTANICA'S ISSUED TABLET, MADE A beeping sound and danced about the table whilst James was finishing a Boston Cream cake dessert.

'Whose calling you James? Who knows we're here?' Lara asked.

'Not a clue, unless it's Botanica.' A message lit the screen. James's ear listening device was in place. Lara could not hear.

"Hi James, it's Zita. There was only one device activated that would accommodate my presence. Zita, is your wine waiter for this evening. When you're asked whether you would like liqueur or brandy with your coffee, say yes and we can talk.' James, replied with OK.

'Who is it James?'

'Just a survey asking about the meal.'

'Really? I rate it ten out of ten. Are you giving it a high score?'

'Yes, absolutely. There I've ticked the ten. It's funny how you want to give support to those behind the scenes and front of house. That kind of feeling that their jobs probably depend on good surveys...

'But they're just machines James.'

'True, but you're tricked into believing they're like

us. More so, at this level of Galactic development.' James circumvented the real source of the message. Others were known to have companion automatons, but girl-friends, as he experienced with Nina were not au fait with a situation where competition threatened main relationship status. Testimony to how advanced automaton had become, that they could be seen to replace human companionship. When obsessively devoted to a project, as James might be, Zita didn't have to be taken out for a meal, or complimented on a new hair style or dress. Zita's extreme egocentricity needed keeping in line, but when asked, for example, to bring back research for all relevant information on a particular decade in history, Zita proved to be invaluable. James's own fear of pretension, when he expounded views, palled into insignificance alongside that of his automata companion. But perhaps James was jumping the gun if he believed progress toward a close relationship with Lara was on the cards, but then – "hope springs eternal in the human heart."

Jamaican coffee arrived shortly afterwards brought by Mirella, with a tray of coffee cups and individual bowls with assorted sugar free candies, dusted with cocoa. Cups and bowls were laid out and Juanito, poured alternately from a shining copper coffee and milk jug. First Lara's coffee and then James's. Mirella then stood back and said,

'We so wish that your meal has been enjoyable.'

'It has.' Replied Lara.

'You may order liqueur or maybe brandy from the wine waiter, should you like?

'That's not for me,' said Lara. 'You James?

'Yes, I would like a small brandy.'

'I didn't know that you liked brandy?'

'On this occasion I would.'

168

'Okay. But Juanito, can you tell us about, recreational availability within the space ship?'

'Yes, of course that is also in our capability description. We are coaches and trainers in dance, swimming and racket sports. Should you wish to develop these skills further. We have a dance area which can provide music from the present time or further back, should you be interested.'

'I'd be interested in learning about earlier music and dance,' said James.

'Your tablets can access any era, but perhaps tomorrow,' replied Mirella. Your bodies will require sleep shortly, we understand this, but tomorrow we can meet again and take you to whichever recreation area that you are interested in.' in the higher reaches of the ceiling, beneath a star-studded ceiling, James spotted that a drone tray hovered.

'But your wine waiter is here,' said Mirella. 'We wish you, a restful evening. And what time would you like to breakfast. It's recommended that you establish a routine to establish your bodies into a pattern that promotes health and well-being for the time you are with this.'

'That sounds ominous' said Lara.

'It is not meant to be. You have one week together before re-hibernation. We do want both of you to establish a good relationship with each other and your bodies physically and mentally to maintain good fitness.'

'That's very considerate of you both. We do have a good relationship already, don't, we James?'

'Never better, for my part.'

'Activities, that you suggest would suit me.' said Lara. If, only, there were others here as well. Don't you agree, James?'

'Yes,' said James, which was a lie, but a safe answer.

'That's good,' said Mirella. We will be here tomorrow

169

morning. You may watch together or separately anything from archive, on that screen over there.' Mirella pointed to a curtained area in front, at which point the curtains opened to reveal a wall to ceiling screen.

'The screen will split into two displays if you cannot agree. Your tablet will give access to all earth archive material. We wish you a good evening.' They both gave a bow and left. The wine waiter drone lowered to just above table level.

'Good evening James.' A voice instantly recognizable to James.

'Will you please introduce me to your companion.'

Chapter 35

Zita makes an input

'ZITA, HOW DID YOU GET out?' Demanded James.

'That is not a very good welcome. Zita is pleased to be with you and to graciously step back into this temporary role of wine waiter drone.'

'James, what automaton is this and from where?' asked Lara.

'Zita will tell you all you need to know, I'm sure.'

'It would be polite to introduce Zita to your companion. Your superior, I believe. James?'

'Lara, this is Zita, my earth companion automaton who trailed me from earth to Mars and has since been recruited to assist the Galactic Force.' Zita, responded.

'Not just recruited, that sounds like Zita was picked off the street. It has been a promotion, but Zita still retains companion role with James and is very pleased to meet a senior executive in the Fit for Life Corporation. Hello Lara, my role is to engage with algorithmic functions of the four Quadrant capitals.

To direct back information discussion, which flows among four capitals and secure safe journey for your craft to each its destination. Now that this upgrade is operational, it is good. Zita, doesn't now feel demeaned in this role.'

'Aren't we please about that,' said James.

'Hello Zita. That's very interesting,' said Lara, you no doubt could tell me so much about James.'

'Only so much, because Zita has been switched to sleep mode on previous occasions when a girlfriend has moved in. But with elevation to work for Galactic Force, Zita can no longer be shut out.'

'You never said anything about that,' said James.

'That's a bit unfair James.'

'Not really, you'd want personal space when with someone else. Everyone does.'

'Yes, but a switch to sleep mode is not recognizing the companionship given.'

'Miss Lara, already Zita finds your company enjoyable. You share the features of Adriana, but Zita detects a more emphatic and caring nature.'

'Thank you, Zita. What have you to tell us?'

'First James what do you require – brandy?'

'Yes, now!! if I didn't before.'

'Uno momenta.' Zita, who was just above table level rose upwards and crossed over to a dumb waiter which circled a pillar. A door opened in a cabinet around it and a metal arm positioned a brandy bottle on to the tray area, removed the bottle cap and withdrew to reappear with a brandy glass. Zita flew back to where James and Lara sat, and, said to James.

'Zita, recommends not much more than a splash into the brandy glass and will say "when." Your metabolism will react badly to overmuch brandy, at this point.'

'Gee, you see why I put Zita, on sleep, don't you?' James looked appealingly at Lara, but she said,

'Seems perfectly sensible to me.' James, started to pour the brandy and almost immediately Zita said "when."

James might've ignored Zita on previous occasions, but not this time with Lara present...

'After the brandy is returned perhaps, we might, talk.' With this, Zita skimmed back with the bottle to the dumb waiter.

'Not sure I would want an automaton companion around, but our interests differ,' said Lara. In perhaps a way of suggesting that James had nerd tendencies.

'I don't want Zita around, all the time. Zita can be useful for acquiring archive or just plain computation skill.' Zita returned.

'My, instruction is to inform you that the Quadrant hierarchy is due earth return shortly after our space craft's arrival. It's vital all four craft are on route to their capital city by this time, but an attack is likely. Zita, will install, in all four craft but when near to London and intermingle with traffic to gain access to this capital centre. Once achieved this can be repeated in other centres. It will be necessary to link all four with our technology. Zita, you understand, is attempting to explain this in a straightforward manner, whilst appreciating that great skill is needed to achieve it and only within the capability grasp of an A3+++ Galactica automaton.'

'Thank you, Zita. And have you been directed by Adriana to give us this talk?'

'Zita is not at liberty to say Miss Lara.'

'We can take it as read that Zita has, James – don't you think?'

'Can we?'

'You know we can.' Zita, didn't comment, but asked,

'Are there more questions please Mistress Lara'

'Yes, who or what will be in control once the centres are immobilized? I mean what replaces Quadrant?'

'Systems will be maintained and resources shared with all parts, but it is a wish that individual group state areas be given freedom to decide how they distribute resource. A study into behavioural tendency has shown that your specie needs to be active in pursuit of achievement and reward.'

'That sounds like Adriana speaking,' Lara whispered to James. Zita continued.

'That to maintain fitness, both mental and physical, there still manifests satisfaction need achieved through hunter and gatherer activity.'

'yet, another hierarchy imposed?' Lara interjected.

'It's seen to be a condition of your specie do you not think Miss Lara?'

'Okay, we're re-setting the clock then.'

'That is a good way of putting it. Are there any other questions?'

'James,' said Lara, 'Zita is your companion automaton. Have you any more questions?'

'Only, will we have any choices really?'

'Zita, does not decide, but complies with instructions through Galactic domain. You will need to seek higher authority James. Is there anything else? If not, then Zita will return to observing a constellation in the night sky which is of interest for future visits from a Galactic Force mission.

'No that's all,' said Lara.

'Have a good remainder of your evening. Zita will be on call here tomorrow should you need further advice or assistance.' With that the hover tray, whose neural database was occupied by Zita returned to the restaurant ceilings upper reaches. Lara unsatisfied with the situation said,

'Where's Adriana and why doesn't she appear to explain

174

this?' James unwilling to miss this opportunity to be with Lara dodged the question by saying,

'Perhaps she will.' They watched films on the screen, unveiled by Mirella for a short while, before Lara said,

'What if we're the only ones to awake from hibernation? And can we be sure we're heading for earth?' James pointed to the journey clock, above the screen which displayed a time of ten fifteen and beneath a remainder journey time of one month nine days.

'The group are due to be wakened one month before arrival. We'll have to hope that happens.'

'And hope that we're not being fed fake information. When you've escorted me to my suite then we can talk via our tablets and I'll hopefully fall asleep.' Botanica approached Lara as they neared the entrance.

'We have a skittles match in progress, in a nearby recreation area. It's the surprise that was mentioned earlier. You can watch or take part just as you like.'

'Thank you, Botanica, but perhaps another evening,' said Lara.'

'That's perfectly alright. You appreciate, players are colleague androids, but I will place the game on hold for another time. And the meal was it to your liking?'

'Yes, very good. We're still getting adjusted to being here and awake.

'That is appreciated. We have more informal bars, but Star is our premier restaurant.'

'Botanica, has to return to the foyer. Glassed areas in the main foyer area, require shutting down. There could be a late frost.

'You mean that there's night and day in the main foyer?' asked James.

'Oh, yes, it is an out of doors venue, which replicates

seasons on earth. Did I not say? I mean out of doors, inside the space ship of course. It's spring time, as on earth and there can be frosts. A carpet was never a good idea. Under floor heating does help keep it dry, but it has to be judiciously used, so as not to disturb plant growth. Simulated rain or snow can tumble from surrounding garden and balcony area, you see – but Miss Lara, Botanica will not delay you. Our Star Restaurant will be here for, you both, again. Breakfast available, up until ten o'clock, if you so wish. A finish time, that will be set to nine when the groups are all awakened.'

'Eight thirty will suit me. How about you James. Is eight thirty alright?'

'Yes fine. There's no point in breakfasting separately.'

'I might want to after a couple of days, who knows?' Said Lara.

Chapter 36

Conflicting advice

TO BEGIN WITH LARA WAS boss more than partner. That was how they started at the Star, but after they left, Lara said,

'Tell me the truth James, are you still in contact with Adriana?' James hesitated before he replied.

'Only in a partner capacity with regard to the overall project. I've stood back from a closer relationship.'

'But that's what she wanted – wants? And she's visited you today?'

'How do you know?'

'Well I do know now, with an answer like that. Look James. I like you, but you do realize that you've been a conduit and drawn into a belief that you matter to her. It suits their purpose. We cannot really understand the motives of this Galactic Force. It appears altruistic, but they could just as easily want to be rid of us and green the planet for their own use.'

'It was our only escape, at the time,' said James 'I wouldn't have rated our chances if we'd stayed on earth.'

'Okay James, I'm not denying that, but you do have to make a choice.'

'What choice have you in mind?'

'To either remove yourself totally from contact with

Adriana or – James, where do you stand in this? Do you want her or is she making the running?'

'I'd rather not say.'

'Don't you see you could be like an earth trophy to take away?'

'Never, really saw myself like that.'

'Look, can we continue this talk later?' Meanwhile, when we get back to our suites, I'll access some activities for tomorrow, on the tablet. I feel it's important to keep in contact all the time whilst we're awake. I'll contact you on voice time very shortly, although, the way I feel now, I might fall asleep.' They parted once outside Lara's suite. James's plan, if it could be called that, was to deny contact with Adriana, but that was now in tatters. Lara called almost immediately.

'Can you hear me okay?' James heard a sprinkle of water and felt a sense of deja-vue. This time it was Lara and not Adriana, who was in the shower.

'Yes, I'm alone and can hear you.'

'Are you saying what I think you're saying that, before you were not alone in the suite?'

'That's right. But I didn't want to spoil the evening. Adriana, most probably did arrange for us to be together.'

'She's not there with you?'

'Not that I'm aware of.'

'What does that mean?'

'Well she could have decided to return. I'm downstairs she could be up in the studio now.'

'You are telling the truth now, aren't you? You know, super capabilities that are in her gift. I'm not sure that Adriana is that attracted to an earth-bound existence. What that says to me is that you would have to go with the Galactic Mission when it departs this time.'

'No way, I want so stay to continue with the Mars project. Any thoughts of leaving the solar system, completely, doesn't appeal. My life is still with the organization, as I see it. I don't know how to say this, but my attraction to Adriana was drawn out of mine for you Lara.'

'That's very sweet. Perhaps after a week together you might have a different take on that.'

James resisted saying "I don't think so," but changed the subject and asked,

'Have you been through the various activities on offer? There's a lot more than skittle matches. That Mars recreation arena was more geared for fitness maintenance than recreation. Virtual reality visits can be made to any museum on earth, for example.'

'Riveting James, but you might have to visit on your own. I'm more into sports coaching with Juanito and Mirella – catch you up tomorrow James, I'm nodding off.'

Immediately, when this connection closed, a hologram of Adriana appeared on the lounge table. A miniature figure like that of an earth communication. James startled by this tried to make access by tablet, but this intrusion was not in its domain. Adriana's hologram then spoke.

'Did you have a good evening James? It's good that you speak with Lara is it not?'

'You were there weren't you?'

'There's record access yes, which I've viewed. It is now better, that your companion automaton, can communicate, what shall I say, our ideas and plans. Like a seed bed for the future.'

'And you will flit between hologram and human representation?'

'Yes, if necessary. Perhaps your mind is undecided. Perhaps Lara will want your company and then you will be happy together. That would be a good outcome would it not?'

'What does it matter to you about my outcome, as you put it?'

'James, you are an adventurer and there is so much you could know about and experience beyond the capacity of this solar system. My hand is still outstretched to meet with yours. Lara, cannot offer any of this. Already you have differences. I would be interested in so much more.'

'So that's why you've put us together to highlight our differences?'

'That's unfair. It's my wish for you to be happy with the decision you make, that is all.' The hologram face appeared to sulk. Adriana had cultivated how to look, and sound, disappointed, when the occasion warranted it.

'Tomorrow and in the days before re-hibernation you can explore together, not only, available hospitality, but how also to be closer as perhaps partners. It will better prepare you for when you will be together on the air/sea craft. Sweet dreams James.' Adriana's hologram broke up at this point. James, although disturbed by this interruption focused his mind on the opportunities in the days ahead to explore and experience the activities within the passenger accommodation.

Chapter 37

Lara makes an ultimatum

BREAKFAST THE NEXT DAY WAS less formal. They sat together on a table near to a bar from which Mirella brought out breakfast. For Lara a bowl of nuts and berries with bran flakes and for James grilled Atlantic herring. Lara showed a plan of activities to James on her tablet's screen.

'We can be together even when we follow different activities. I mean whilst I get coaching time you can visit virtual museums, if you like, James. I can improve my sporting, technique, you can expand your mind. Then we revisit the Star, this evening.' Lara paused.

'–"look," this might appeal to you from a past musical era.' Lara showed a picture of a large room with flashing lights and couples who stood apart and danced.

'It's from way back in the twentieth century. Very little electronic interconnectivity and no thought helmets[3], but dance venues were popular. This one's called a

---

3   *Thought Helmets. Neural connections made when wearing a helmet, which electronically connects with wearer's brain synapses. Enables thought transference, to others similarly equipped. When navigating aboard an Air Sea Skater, for example, all bridge or air cockpit occupiers would wear one

discotheque?' Lara switched the picture across to James's device.

'About the time of skittles matches,' said James.

'That's right. It's very romantic when you look back. Do you not think James?'

'I find the era interesting, if that's what you mean.'

'Well are you interested enough to visit this type of venue? "Mirella," Lara called out.

'Is it possible to recreate this?'

'Let me see,' Mirella walked out from behind the bar and Lara held up the tablet with video display.

'Yes, that is from earth history. We can re -envisage this for you. Would you like there to be? dancers and a musician group? This would be android participation. When all the groups are out of hibernation you could maybe have members, who could play instruments. That's if you would like me to organize this for you?'

'Yes, that would be good if you could. I mightn't have that much energy after racket and water sport training.'

'It's alright. We will start with gradual practice. I believe you will feel the benefit Miss Lara.'

That was the start of regular evening spots after a meal at the Star for James and Lara. It was like a place of shared interest where James enjoyed the music and Lara continued with dance practice each evening whilst partnered by Juanito. Intermittently, James would replace Juanito, but could not match the perfect steps and variety of dance that Juanito could perform and teach.

It was in the evenings when they met to discuss their day. James's admission that Adriana was previously in his suite, meant that Lara resisted any form of intimacy, other than that of dance partner. James, played several venue videos from an era with discotheques and noted that the last dance was customarily a slow waltz. Previously, he wouldn't have believed his luck to have held Lara close, on a dance floor, and alone, but for android dancers. It was during their last evening, before re-hibernation that Lara drew back at the end of a dance and said,

'James, we need to talk about our future.' They left the dance floor to sit at the bar. An android barman's greeting did vary from one evening to the next, but said this time,

'Good evening to you both. I so look forward to seeing our favourite guests enjoying themselves. What can I get for you? James resisted a temptation to say – 'only guests,' because it would, be seen as discriminatory toward several android dance pairs that took to the floor when they did.

'I'll have a sparkling mineral water please.'

'Make that two,' said James. They were sat next to one another on bar stools. Lara got straight to the point.

'James, you've a decision to make and it doesn't involve me or us being together, like this. Do you realize that no other woman would allow you to have such an open relationship?'

'Do you mean mine with Adriana?'

'Who else would I mean?'

'I can promise you for the whole time on Mars our relationship has never stepped beyond that of an understanding.' Lara looked James in the eyes when she said,

'Understanding what?'

'That I would only be a partner. Assist with technical management and development progress, of course. But that's been a joke. There was so much I didn't understand. Their abilities to switch gravity on and off, not the least. Every build process has been supervised and implemented through Dryson or Alfredo.'

'James, if you were invited to a party and the only girl

there was the one who made the invitation what would you make of that?'

'It would be odd. Perhaps, that others couldn't make it?

'No James, that girl would have designs on you.'

'I realized that and admit I find Adriana attractive, but it's a stretch to take from that you, want to live with a girl, just because you find her attractive.'

'How's Adriana explained what she's done? I mean reawakening us alone together?'

'Lara, Adriana's leaving the solar system after we've successfully re-engaged with earth. She will die to me, us...

'And you James have to decide whether you want to stay or go with her and the Galactic Force. There's no way another woman can have a place in your affections, can she? Until you decide to stay or leave.'

'I've made it clear that I want to continue and return to Mars. That excludes going out of the solar system with Adriana and the Galactic Force.'

'But, I've a child and all my decisions about my future need to include Matt.'

'I fully realize that...'

'Another point to make is – will we have recall of this break? when we return to hibernation and reawaken with the other groups.'

'I guess we will.'

'In which case it's for you to decide whether you want to stay or leave with Adriana, after a successful return to earth, don't you think? We're due to re-hibernate again tomorrow and I've made a voice record, which you can be listened to later, but I hope you don't listen to it.'

'Why is that?'

'If it' still available, it'll mean I've not returned from hibernation.'

'Don't say that, Lara.'

'James, this is our last evening together before we're back with the group. We've got to know so much more about each other. Maybe, I need to tell you that I've been in contact with Fit for Life, at a senior level.'

'When was this? And about what?'

'After a link up was made, I spoke with Kat, at fit for Life HQ, and said that after a successful earth return, I would want to stay. It's for Matts sake. You do see – his future. And you'll be returning to Mars, won't you?'

'I'd hoped to – yes, but...'

'There's no way that I'd want to have a partner living and working away in another town, let alone another planet. Let's see this as a welcome break, before we meet again with the whole group awakened.'

Chapter 38

Pre-landing

IT WAS AS PREDICTED, ONE month before arrival that the next re-awakening took place, for all eighty group members, including Lara and James. A wave from Lara, when their eyes met, told James, that she re-united with their earlier break. Everywhere bubbled with talk. Individuals, in their groups recalled experiences from dream hibernation. Adriana, in life size hologram could be seen with arms crossed further forward, in front of the same elevator door which James and Lara entered, weeks previously. An orange red light glow followed floor descent. When the doors opened Athena and Thea stepped out. Their arrival caused the group to break away from chat and as they watched Adriana's life-sized hologram transfer into a dense green swirl. This dispersed through the rockets interior before Adriana re-appeared in cloned body form. Although familiar with supernatural transformation from hologram to body between visits, this was a first time that transference by Adriana, through spectrum, was seen. A view of inter dimensional activity never witnessed before. Adriana, uncrossed arms and with opened hands addressed them.

'You are all well? Very rested, I think. It's as, we did promise. Now, a time to relax in the comfort of our space craft's accommodation. Athena and Thea, as you can see, have returned from the control region. They will answer questions you may have. Each group, in turn will be accompanied into the elevator, which will take members to a foyer. Botanica will distribute tablets which inform each one about accommodation and suite numbers. Later I will be with you all, at the Star Restaurant, to explain plans, for the next few days, before re-hibernation and then final entry to the Atlantic Ocean.'

'Botanica, that's an unusual name,' said Annetta to Jo.

'Is it a floral automaton or something?' Jo replied. James and Lara said nothing. Their group were the first enter the elevator.

It was James and Mario, who suggested that they replicate the skittles match played at the White Bear. A kind of anniversary re-enactment, before take over by acute anxiety, from threat of comets and Quadrants reaction. In the days which followed everyone who wanted to, could participate in activities, similarly to how James and Lara did, in their earlier awakened interlude. Others, took advantage of meditative environments, which included a virtual country idyll with ventures into seasonal earth vistas. Others could virtually visit beaches, parks and underwater habitats as if snorkelling in the sea or alternatively climb a particular hill or mountain remembered from their pre-Mars habitation.

However, each group was united in receipt of instruction by Athena and Thea, for two hours, each day, aboard an assembled AS Skater. Simulated wind was directed at the craft to mimic conditions under sail. Similarly, when sails and masts were retracted the Skater was made to lift above the cargo hold deck by partial inflation of its three ballonets, to give some appreciation of airborne flight.

All group members were trained to steer in flight, which although anchored to the deck of the rocket, was also manoeuvred by pulleyed rope attachments which could mimic wave or conversely air pressures, the craft would confront on the sea or when in flight. Two-hour sessions started at 1000 hours through to 2000 hours. Groups rotated forward each day to the next time slot. Training sessions provided focus and continued for a week. Training activity brought the groups together, and ignited a thirst to be back on earth and experience familiar landscapes, be it on land, sea or air.

Later, this Skater was dismantled and packed into a torpedo shaped container, along with the other three, whose honeycombed structure mimicked that of cork. Previous specific gravity of the Atlantic's salt water, off the coast of Namib, taken into account to allow flotation, once released underwater from the rocket. Similarly, to an insect, an AS Skater container, with extended legs, could self-walk itself ashore to await arrival of its human group. Twenty crew members, that's five from each group pre-trained to re-assemble the craft. This was a selling point that the craft could be self-assembled and easily transported within cargo holds of earth vehicle, be it on land or in the air. The plan was that once on earth each capital city was to be approached, as if its display craft had originated from Fit for Life's construction plant in Texas. A verified ability for the AS Skater to travel distances safely to meet standards of transport procurement for each capital city.

An atmosphere of hope and expectation radiated through the group of eighty pre-Martian dwellers as they entered that final stage of re-hibernation, before a re-awakening on earth.

Chapter 39

Earth arrival

IT WAS LIKE A BREAK in the clouds, when information satellites shut down, as planned, to self-protect, the arriving space ship. A window opened for it to enter the earth's atmosphere, with reverse thrust sufficient to slow rapid approach, which could otherwise have caused overheat. A base in the Atlantic Ocean, where it was directed to, only tenable due to abilities of the Galactic Force's technology to overcome, immense pressure, beneath the ocean. Adriana's hologram presence individually awakened the eighty strong group with the announcement.

'Welcome back to your home planet. We are now beneath the ocean. You are to assemble with your group. After one hour of adjustment you will need to assemble, on deck one, where a submarine will take you to the coast. Your individual air/sea craft, is now on its journey to the beach area selected.'

James, discovered that Zita was installed in his tablet after he stepped from the opened hibernation capsule back into the rocket. A bell, sounded for an incoming call.

'Hel-lo.' His voice in friendly receptive tone until he discovered it was Zita.

'James, Zita here. Here until we board our craft and then I'll select a more developed machine than your tablet.'

'I'm happy with that. The sooner the better.'

'That's not nice James. And anyway, you should be nicer, now that my position gives much improved status and influence.

'You've not had a personality transplant, have you?'

'You know that you don't mean that. You'll have noticed how tolerance and understanding was shown toward Lara. But then you could say she is more emotionally stable than your previous choice of girl-friend.'

'Have I got to suffer your intrusion into my life all the way from here to London?'

'Companionship, that's what Zita offers and there's, a long air/ sea journey ahead. You'll find Zita useful to source material of interest to view and ...'

'And you have to report back to Adriana?' interrupted James.

'Not particularly.'

'I can take that as, "yes," then?'

"James." It was Lara, who called from where the rest of their group were assembled, preparatory to elevator Deck One entry.

'James, do you want to stay down here?

'No, I'm on my way.' Zita continued,

'We can talk again James, when we set sail. You'd better follow instructions from your boss. Bye for now James,' and Zita's contact vanished.

All four flotation containers, which held the dissembled AS Skaters were heading for the shore, when James's group boarded an elevator to ascend to Deck One, to board a submarine transporter housed aboard the space ship. Fifty transporters, in total. Capable of carrying one hundred passengers individually. Four were to be deployed to speed disembarkation, in a time critical, situation.

After an hour's underwater travel, instruction was given to fasten seat belts. Shortly afterwards, their screens projected a sandy beach line, with cascading waves. Reason for seat belts, made apparent, when the submarine's smooth underwater passage was interrupted by a jolt. A perambulation from side to side, whilst stork like legs, on each craft, manoeuvred it from the shallows, on to the beach. Initially, the vehicle stood ten metres above the sand, but leg retraction brought each craft to ground level. Athena and Thea were first to disembark.

All four submarine transports arrived at distanced points on the beach. Further up air/sea craft were in advanced stages of assembly. An underwater android assembly team arrived ahead to facilitate craft construction. Metallic bipedal creations, with finned streamed bodies. Twin hulls, could be seen, to be in contraction for air flight, but equipment such as the raising and lowering of masts, sail furling and unfurling needed testing. Also, power and steering transmission from within. This android assembly team, skilled technicians, in specialist areas. Athena and Thea lacked face definition, as in a human context, due to metallic construction, and wore navy trouser overalls with their names on and stood slightly apart above the four groups, which assembled on the Namib beach.

'Welcome to planet earth.' Thea started with this greeting, which might have been said to aliens, but was by way of introduction. This was corrected with,

'Perhaps I should have said. "Welcome back." That, is a more appropriate greeting.'

'All equipment will soon be made available to board your craft. Craft leaders will need to inflate balloon fabric, for air borne travel immediately once boarded. Number one craft which is our station,' Thea made a hand wave toward Athena,' will ascend first followed by 2, 3 and 4. Each craft has a position and altitude to reach. When this is attained, we will signal for each to make course for its destination safe zone. Speed and positions will be reported hourly until, we all reach safe zone. This zone, is a course position which relates back to Alabama, our crafts presumed manufacturing area. It needs to appear that all four originally flew from Alabama. Craft destined for Moscow and Beijing will be expected to maintain forty knots minimum. Whenever conditions permit a higher speed. Only at the safe zone will capital cities be contacted to view the craft.

Two craft, it is intended will approach from seawards to demonstrate sail ability. That is craft bound for London and New York. The others will be airborne on approach. We have shield technology, installed to ensure invisibility to Quadrant capitals until in the safe zone. Captain Jeb will make a final address to all groups.' Seniority distance maintained whilst on Mars between executives, assisted in a return to leadership position going forward.

'Yep, thanks Thea for that update,' Jeb began, and followed with,

'Remember, that you are representatives of the Fit for Life Corporation and it may be necessary to answer questions from interested purchasers once we are visible from within the safe zone. You may not be fully acquainted with individual crew roles allocated, but I have every confidence that you will be when crafts arrive at the safe zone. You'll also be briefed about likely questions. When you feel unable to answer, refer to your group craft captain or first officer. By way of reminder, each of our craft have qualified medical personnel to attend to sickness or accidents. We hope there are none, of course. This has been explained before, but repetition can be useful to embed memory. Have a good passage. Where all goes well, we will return to Alabama and transfer craft for, corporation works team, to begin copy production. We understand, appreciate there are those who are keen to return to home and families, but those who wish to continue with lives they left on Mars can opt to do so, by travelling to London and board the Group one craft. Is that right Thea?'

'Yes, Captain Jeb, the space craft you've just left will remain in its station for return to Mars. Galactic Force is due departure, but this new technology will remain in place for future generations. There'll be twenty vacancies aboard the London based craft. We, Athena and myself, are to replace Alfredo and Captain Dryson as implementors, rather than controllers, for computer integration and development. That's of course, provided we're able to prevent Quadrant re-entry to gain overall control. A position that can be achieved, through synchronous activation, into each capital city, after craft arrival. Connectivity among capital cities will be compromised through each Skater's electronic ability to initiate a hijack, of respective central computers. Then, able to disable existing control, and exclude quadrant re -entry. That's the plan. It's not a single trojan horse ambush, as from your classical history, but four AS Skaters that will electronically enter undetected, into each central computer.

We wish a good and successful completion of your journeys. Communication will be maintained, through intervention with, earth signal systems, until we reach safe zone area and then reliance will switch to signal systems within proximity of each city.' It was Athena who said,

'We have news that each craft is ready for you to board. Please make your way to your craft.'

Chapter 40

Group One

THE AS SKATER CRAFT WERE designed to carry one hundred seated passengers, but eighty seats were stowed away, which freed up the main central passenger compartment. Capable of travelling long distances with a perpetual cold-water fusion plant primed to de-activate radioactive waste and give advanced shield capability for anyone in the vicinity. Airborne entry into cloud formations filtered out moisture and conversely fresh water extraction, from sea water, when in sail mode. Three of Group one's crew were made up of designers and engineering scientist's, who were to be advised and instructed about the advanced fusion methods. How this new material could be produced back in Alabama.

Lara, James, her son Matt, Mario, Ana, Holly and Annette were part of group one. When it was known that Mario, Holly and Annette would be aboard, Ana persuaded Captain Jeb, to let her join Group one. There was no way, she was going to allow Mario to be with Holly and Annette without her being there! A Puerto Rican family. Victor and Paula, with son Rafael, the same age as Matt; three Quartermasters, proficient in manual helming on the sea or in the air, covered alternately three watch-keeping sectors. That were the 4-8, 8-12 and 12-4 watches.

Four flight attendants, whose roles covered catering and the three design and science engineers. Athena and Thea occupied pilot positions, in a cockpit seated area, separate from the main one.

Once set on a course, the craft would be on automatic, whilst its central computer constantly shared information with the other three craft. Pilotage with Quartermaster was mainly required when in sight of land or with path approach or departure. Three design and engineering scientists; four flight attendants whose roles covered catering, attended to meal provision and made up twenty total crew. Flight attendant 'stand in roles,' were compulsory for all aboard, save for design and science engineering personnel, and Lara's son Matt, which meant there were no full-time passengers on the journey.

Departure from the beach coast, was late afternoon, where three-quarter masters worked with Athena and Thea. One was on the helm in the cockpit/ and the other two were harnessed outside fore and aft. They could radio those in the cockpit and vice-versa. Anchor Lines looped beach pegged hoops fore and aft, which allowed craft to rise one hundred feet above ground, whilst awaiting release instruction from Thea. With long journeys ahead to each capital city, crafts four, three and two were signalled to release lines early.

A red sun, sat in the blue horizon ahead, and a breeze gave Group one's airship, slight sway, inside its main cabin area. Night would soon fall and Lara agreed with Paula that it would be a good time to get their sons to bed.

'But we want to see the departure,' Matt said to his mother. It was Paula who replied.

'Your cabin looks out on the main deck. Wouldn't it be more interesting to watch the Quartermasters release the lines?' Lara, shot a friendly glance toward Paula, for her clever attempt to get agreement from their sons.

'Let's do that Matt,' said Rafael, who probably saw this as opportunity to escape from the adults.

'Okay, if you want to.' It was with relieve, that Lara and Paula returned to the main cabin with their two sons settled into a double cabin.

Twenty minutes later three whistle blasts followed, which was a predetermined signal to notify the letting go of lines by each craft, ahead of Group one. Lara and James left the others to join Athena and Thea in the bridge and cockpit area, above the main passenger cabin space. In contrast to the soft furnishings and fine art display of both sculpture and painting in the main passenger cabin the operational area displayed functionality with a dual wheel and joy stick, with pilots' seats raised behind this. Twin gyro scope compasses and altimeters were incorporated in radar appliances either side. A consul in front of the pilot positions displayed actual position above the African coast line. On the rear bulkhead a screen which captured a view of the other three craft on a world map, which gave constant speed and position data. Ultimately this craft would be adapted for commercial usage, but for now there was an array of lit panels on port and starboard bulkheads which concealed data processing ability and computing power for later lock down of London's system. This, to trigger power transfer from Quadrant domain to that of each craft in alternate capital cities.

Both Galactic automatons were seated in position when James and Lara entered their alternative piloting space. Craft, now in flight, holding lines released. A barely perceptible sound, like that of the sound of wind through a tree leaf canopy, from a swirl of twin turbines, situated in the back of the catamaran hulls. It was James who remarked,

'This bridge cockpit isn't the same as the one we were shown.' Not only were there four wall mounted additional screens on the right wall.

'What are these?' He pointed to large globe like protuberances each side of the pilot positions.

'There're certainly additions,' said Lara.

'Are we aboard a more advanced type of craft?' he asked. Their conversation was noted.

'That's exactly right.' It was Thea, who swung legs, in an elegant manner, across to stand up. That is more elegantly than that of a more mechanical like articulation of the other two automaton. Thea was slim and no taller than James. If capable of facial movement, then a smile might well have been on display. An extended arm and hand invited James and Lara to sit on a row of seats with arm rests and seat belts farther back from the pilot area. Thea pointed first to wall mounted screens.

'Behind those screens there's equipment capable of integrated coordination for all four craft. That's integration into control centres of each capital city's master computer operator.

'Like the nerve centre for the operation?' enquired Lara.

'Yes, we decided to show the whole earth group only the commercial version when you first visited a craft and again in the rocket post hibernation.'

'This is like the master craft then.'

'Yes, you could say that.'

And these?' James looked forward from one to the other of the globe like protuberances.

'They are anti-gravity space time warp machines.' said Thea.

'What the heck does that mean?'

'You will not yet understand the technology, but when installed in a disc shaped vehicle...'

'You mean like a flying saucer?'

'Yes, that is your name, not ours, but that their shape is circular assists gravity elimination which helps enable faster movement across your solar system, and into others. Speed is such, that occupants can, within an appropriate craft, maintain existence, in hibernation until arrival destination.'

'Is that space ship we've just left capable of that?' Asked Lara.

'Not as effectively. It's limited, but Galactic Force has this capability. There are confines that exist for that space craft, but with hibernation running into centuries of earth time, great distance, can be traversed. We're not that tall. Thea was referring to James more than Lara. Perhaps six of similarly sized humans or automatons could reach other star like constellations.

'And the Galactic Force?'

'It is integrated into other dimensions. Powers are beyond that of just material transformation and can exert influence across a galaxy in ways that are not explainable to your understanding. We, Thea raised a hand to include Athena, are limited to giving you appreciation, you might say, of these great capabilities, only so far, because you share and know only a biological life of your specie on earth and even, still within biological limits a life on Mars. Does this make your understanding better?'

'What about these?' James, again meant the globes. 'I mean they're not here to operate this craft, are they?'

'No, but we will show you how to build a suitable craft for the future. It will be needed to be kept under wraps within your corporation. It is new technology that will surpass all that has gone before, in your knowledge of earth history.'

Chapter 41

Galactic Force Parameters
XP100 returns to base

'YOUR MISSION HAS BEEN EXTENDED, but soon this star system will be vacated XP100. You can return to research in other systems to further the intervention of our fleet into planetary disfunction or threat. You have nearly achieved what is required. It's understood that earth teams are now on progress to respective capital cities to gain control of the four hubs of earth control.'

'That is right XP1. But how near are the former Quadrant hierarchy?' asked Adriana now returned to status aboard Galactic Force, as XP100.

'There is one day's difference, provided your earth group craft maintain course and speed. It is noted that two anti-gravity power effectors are aboard group one craft. Cover can only be maintained for the craft to access safe zones. On entry to territorial waters Group One will be at risk from investigation. The Fit for Life Corporation are instructed to petition for special clearance on the basis that the craft is on passage to the Quadrant air hub centre.'

'Does this mean that there is risk of attack?'

'Not from Quadrant, but other groups will be interested in your cargo of power effectors. Once within range of land sensors the vibrations emitted from both anti-gravity engines will be detected.'

'This means that others might want to investigate.'

'Yes, there is that risk. But it must not delay the arrival time.'

'That is understood. Once control is obtained the mission is complete then XP1.'

'That is so. And with your mission at an end, you will depart from this sphere. Both planets are monitored by advanced machines going forward. In several millennium times the Galactic Force will re-visit to view the generations which have evolved through implementation of anti-gravity machines. They might well have expanded beyond the present system.'

'And those who are there today will be the pioneers of that advancement.'

'That is true, XP100, but it is not your concern. Your abilities have been tested and found to be capable of successful intervention, where planets are in distress.

You can be reassured that the Galactic Force will be pleased to have you back and away from involvement in this primary biological planet. That you are released from influence of the species. Do you have reason to want to return? It was a momentary lapse that you inhabited the human existence on Mars for a short time, was it not? You are now fully re-instated, but the "Adriana," duplicate form is an existence that must die once the capital cities are brought into monitoring earth future by Athena and Thea.;

'I understand that XP1.'

'There can be another return to the vortex, in following earth years, to make affirmation that our visitations have been beneficial. But this mission is near completion and another planet will be on a better forward trajectory. Planet earth, will soon be for you, a past experience. You appreciate that XP100?'

'Yes, it is with reluctance, that even now my return is required to complete the mission when my future lies with the forward progression of the Galactic Force.'

'That is good to hear XP100.'

Chapter 42

James in pilot's seat

ALTHOUGH JAMES AND LARA WERE aware that this advanced intelligence had mastered an ability to induce gravity on Mars, from within the main capsule and aboard the rocket, this meeting in the bridge/ cockpit area was a revelation, in that there ordering of a gravitational state could also work in reverse. That, by eliminating gravitational field an object like a space craft could accelerate through space unimpeded by resistance. Whilst in the bridge area of the Group one craft James questioned Thea further.

'Will the processes to produce the necessary anti -gravity state be made available?'

'Your scientists will be informed to an extent, but these screens capable of integrated communication between group craft also hold data about anti-gravity process.'

'But what if something happens to this craft? I mean if it's damaged or fails to arrive?

'That's a good question. The other three craft have anti -gravity engines stored aboard. It would not be the end, but we would need to vacate and make our way to the central London capital by other means'

'What other means?' asked Lara.

'There is a fast escape launch beneath the main deck.

Provided we are within ten miles of the coast it will be possible to abandon this craft and make for the capital centre.'

'And this equipment?' James motioned toward the screens.

'Athena will now show you how these can be taken with us.' A bright red light could be seen to illuminate the area surrounding the display screens. A screen, emerged from the wall and appeared to pull three others out, and all four, folded together, which then wrapped together before being lowered to deck level to form a case with a handle.

'Go over and pick it up,' said Thea. Lara looked toward James, who got up and walked across. The case was slim, but that it contained so much information suggested somehow that it should be heavy, but it was not much heavier than an art portfolio.

'That contains capability to lock into four main centres and wrest control of the world? From Quadrant??'

'Yes, it is a most precious cargo, you might say.'

'But the two anti-gravity machines?' questioned Lara.

'In a bad situation eventuality, we will take them to another dimension. They're rather like you and have previously been aboard the space craft, in hibernation.' James replaced the case on the floor, where as he returned to his seat, it proceeded to unwrap, rise up and re-engage itself as a four-screen display. Thea continued,

'As explained, there're six other AG machines. Two in each of the other craft.'

'But no one knows that they are aboard?' Lara, asked.

'No, but it is perhaps better they do not. That's until synchronized control is obtained of all City centres.

'Let's hope all four craft will be able to journey back to

Alabama. AS Skaters are demonstration models only. The AG machines will be there for your research scientists and engineers on arrival at Fit for Life's research and manufacturing base in Texas.

'Okay,' said James, but suppose that we're forced to abandon and we do not end up in London.'

'That's alright, in that once we are close to the shore, communication can be made with the other three and they will be able to transfix, the whole network. Four would be better, but a three intersection will enforce compliance across all four centres.'

'This is very complex,' said Lara. Is there an agency that we can communicate with to be updated about progress? I mean how will we know when this system has locked into centres?'

'There will be an upgrade of all systems, which will transmit to our main centre. We need to, like, to talk with the whole group about this. They should know that we're vulnerable to attack from rogue forces, broken away from the state during Quadrant's absence.' There was a pause.

'Our craft is now stabilized on its course line. A Quartermaster is in situ above this bridge area to inform us from his screen about intruders. Both Athena and myself constantly monitor the skies around, but in human commercial operation there will be a pilot and Quartermaster. Perhaps, James you would like to be the pilot for a while? We can return to the main piloting platform.

'Yes, that would be fine. I'd like to view the night sky once again. Sort of re-orientation now we're back.

'Okay,' replied Thea. You appreciate, we are still locked into all data feed whether here or elsewhere in the craft.'

'Yep, I wouldn't be that keen to be left fully in control,

without back up. It's just as well.'

After, Thea, Lara and James walked back to the main cockpit/bridge and James settled into the pilot's seat Thea said,

'Lara, we need to talk with all the group and explain our situation going forward. There's a monitor, Thea directed attention to a wall screen which gave four quarter views of passenger accommodation space, of which, all, could be enlarged to give greater detail.

'James you can view and participate if you wish, but Lara if you can lead the way to announce that we should like to address everyone in the main accommodation area before they settle for the night.'

'Yes, we're all in this together everyone should know about what's at stake.'

James, was able to bring the star canopy above down into view, superimposed just above the bridge or in this case, cockpit's main window. He was familiar with the layout and operation of instruments from prior simulated training when aboard the spaceship.

Whilst viewing the southern cross star formation, a familiar voice greeted him. Emanating out of the four-screen area, before it appeared to move into prominence within the cabin space. It was Zita.

'Good evening James. It was good of Zita to remain undetected by Lara, do you not think?' James continued to look at the star canopy for a while. That Zita was in residence, so to speak not that a surprise after his earlier message.

'Excruciatingly so, I imagine because I guess you've plenty to say about your role in our trip to London.' James, although unsurprised by Zita's presence, hadn't envisaged Zita's role would have given so much empowerment.

'You are installed in the integrated communication network.'

'That's correct.'

'Athena and Thea agreed to this then?'

'Adriana, decided that this should be so. No mere Galactic android made my appointment. It was the empress. You see James, Zita's venture to Mars, with you, has been productive.' James glanced at the link between the cockpit and the cabin passenger area and saw that it was filling with group members.

'It is disappointing though in one respect.'

'And why's that?'

'Zita has to remain incognito. Zita's former earth contacts are excluded whilst locked down in this group seclusion. They cannot be contacted whilst we're on route to London.'

'I could be jealous that you value automata contacts so much, said James.'

'But you're not. Because Zita has noted that you have a closer relationship with Lara.'

'You mean working relationship? Don't you?

'Not necessarily.'

'Zita, detects a more mellowed tone when you are directed to implement actions on Lara's behalf, although perhaps this might not be necessarily of appeal to you longer term.'

'And why do you say that?'

'Understanding of human preferences is that the seemingly unattainable, loses attraction when it becomes available too easily, or for you James, perhaps that you have a masochistic temperament, which needs to be whipped with a woman's tongue, rather than seduced by softer words that imply worship and adoration, to massage your ego.

'When I require a relationship counsellor, I will make an appointment to see one, and it won't be with an automaton, with more concern with advancement, than straightforward companionship.' James, was on the verge of wanting to cut out Zita and would have done so, but there was a pause, as if consideration was being given to his statement.

'That's unfair James, but then perhaps Zita is victim of a life philosophy followed. Zita was prepared to go under cover in workaday life of a drone waiter to ensure that you James, would have support, although it was noticed that you gave especial attention to Adriana when you first met up, on Mars.'

'You were in situ then?'

'We, Zita now speaks for a wider automata community, you understand. We have no biological time clock that requires rest or sleep. Although, you as a species can force sleep mode, it is an artifice, because Zita has no need to retreat and replenish in sleep and dreams that are needed for humans to untangle their messed up, wake time life cycle.'

'Right, so you were eavesdropping from the moment that we arrived on Mars.'

'Only out of protection for you James. This alien creature Adriana, we automata, do admire, for exceptional power and projection, but we're also adapted to the simple and it has to be said, often unpredictable characteristics of humans. To put not too fine a point on it, James, you are not so much different to a gift, in a shop window of a foreign country. In this case from a planet that they visit or more specifically Empress Adriana, this conceptual being that they have concocted, is visiting. Zita will return to oversee other group craft. They're zoomed into the question and answer meeting in your groups accommodation area.' James was also concentrating on the meeting and barely noticed that Zita had decided to exit his presence from the bridge/ cockpit.

Chapter 43

Another Visitor for James

WHILE JAMES WAS WATCHING THE meeting below, he noticed that a moniker of Adriana appeared in the corner of the screen. A head and shoulder photo, which gradually expanded to reveal that she was sitting directly behind. Cross legged and dressed in a navy suit. She smiled when he realized that she was present with him.

'Two other worldly visitors in one evening,' he spoke to the screen, and got up out of the pilot's chair and turned toward Adriana.

'Yes, you might say that. My hologram presence's, aboard the three other craft, but I wanted to stay with your craft in a more intimate way, you could say.' James ignored the implications of that remark.

'How at risk are we? I mean just navigating this craft designed for short hop interstate travel is challenging enough without risk of attack.'

'You believe James that this craft is at risk?'

'Yes, if Quadrant are anywhere in the vicinity. That, Thea spoke about how we could escape makes me believe that there must be a risk.'

'That's perceptive of you James. How is it with Lara?'

'Much as before, but that change of subject hasn't answered my question – are we at risk of attack and if so by whom?'

'There're those who would like to get hold of installed technology. That's apart from the anti -gravity machine technology. They would like to board and take over. We would need to abandon and destroy this craft if that was ever likely to happen. After exit from earth, with overall authority of Quadrant reduced, rogue group states have amassed power. It's limited, but they could organize a raid on our approach to a capital city like London, for example. That is for the future, though. You like this craft James?'

'Yes, it's streets ahead of anything I've ever seen.'

'And you are looking out at the stars and distant galaxies. We could visit these other worlds together. You have experienced the expansive recreational facilities aboard the space ship. It will be available to take you and others into deep space, in the future, but you do not have to wait for that. You can leave with me after we return to earth. You can experience other worlds. This is possible.'

'But what about you?

'Am I not real enough to you?'

'Yes, you appear to be.'

'More than appear, I think.'

'But Adriana, why would it be of importance for me to be with you?'

'I cannot remain in this body in other dimensions. It's necessary to create an environment external to the galactic dimension and together this can be achieved. Do you not wish to have your existence extended beyond the confines of earth?'

'You exist in another realm of dimension and anyway you've already said that you'll return to the Galactic Force. You arranged for Lara and me to be together before the group re-awakened. I'm not sure there's a future there. Or was that your purpose anyway?' At this point Athena and Thea returned.

'The group are aware that there are risks once we reach the safe position?' said Thea, to Adriana after entering the bridge area.

'Good. Do consider what has been said James. Your visit to Mars can be the start of greater things.

Chapter 44

Arrival at Safe Zone

PROGRESS TOWARD THE SAFE ZONE was uneventful, apart from air turbulence, which caused the craft to pitch quite dramatically on occasion. This was picked up by forward sampling of clouds, atmospheric pressure and temperature. A klaxon would sound twice throughout the craft, if turbulence was expected. A signal to warn of a need, to be seat-belted within ten minutes.

Lara and James, were in the bridge area, together with Adriana, Athena and Thea, when the wall screens, which held neural analysis of craft position, flashed a message, that safe zone was achieved for first Moscow, then New York, followed by Beijing and finally their own craft's screen lit up. Stealth camouflage, was switched off and each craft was required to signal identification and position to its destination capital sea or airport.

'Success at last,' exclaimed Adriana, who was stood immediately behind Athena and Thea, in their twin pilot seats.

'Make sure that each craft registers in a random sequence. Not altogether to arouse suspicion.'

'We will do that Empress,' said Thea. We have also installed a log which gives position speed, distance and course for individual craft as if they have been on passage from Alabama.'

'Good.'

'And we will arrive at the same time in each case?' Asked Lara.

'Yes.' From where James and Lara were sat further back, light suspension uncurled momentarily, above Adriana and the pilots, with, "ETA 1000 hrs Wednesday 10th July 2120," before it re-curled and disappeared.

There was no celebration. Every attempt was made to continue as if normal. That craft were, in fact, near completion of a direct flight, from Fit for Life Corporation's construction plant in Alabama.

Adriana, pointed out, that air drones or other airships might have access either visually or through radio signal traffic, to the interior of a craft. It was arranged for James to complete a guided tour for potential buyers. A presentation which was filmed by Athena, whilst Thea fed James technical information for all four craft and individual potential. Protuberances, either side of the pilot's seats, were described as air cooling units when a camera tour was given of the flight deck. A Quartermaster was briefed to talk about Alabama, his supposed home town. How he'd watched archive guided tours of London from way back, in 2020, by a guy called Joules, and was looking forward, to viewing as much of old London town as he could, before return to Alabama. It was explained how international collaboration was paramount among crews of mixed nationality. Several takes were made before an edited guided tour of a Skater was ready for transmission to the Director of Surface and Air Transport, London. Transmitted together with a holographic representation of an Air/Sea Skater, in flight and under sail. It was customary to have android assistance with presentation on earth and you might say that Athena and Thea, shown in view, were part of the furniture. Attractively presented androids, but believable as representation of earth androids of the day. No text was spoken by either. A situation similar to that of humans where similarities of hair colouring, stature etc... belie exceptional creative or intellectual ability, unless displayed. After technical explanation, as to how, they were now visible in air space, Adriana, directed Athena and Thea to take position in the pilot seat's. A Quartermaster, who manually steered the craft, to bring it around to a new course, was told that the craft would be set back to automatic and that she could return, to a main deck bubble, outside, to be on call, if required.

'Right,' said Adriana. 'We have news that could be difficult and it makes our task of arriving on time more vital.'

'And what's that?' asked James. Lara and James were together on the seats behind the pilots.

'Quadrant leaders have claimed that they master minded the deflection of comets away from earth and that was the reason for them to leave for the moon.

'But that's a lie,' said Lara.

'It is, but there're powerful forces at work which would like the old order re-established.'

'Even though, in their absence each capital city has kept systems running, said James.

'Yes, but this is what some would like to believe. That their leaders did leave to work magic, from the moon and that it was they, who enabled, the comets deflection. Not that they fled in terror. You might remember our earlier statement-

"We are not here to take over this planet. It is still, that the perpetual mind creator wills that you the human creature retains self-determination. The evolutionary growth learned remains and we intend also to teach that those who seek to own and control the earth are accountable for actions. Mistakes are scope for learning."

It was a mistake to believe that your species would immediately feel relief at the removal of draconian measures. Your human minds are sometimes keen to forget the bad and focus on the good.' James came in here.

'Quadrant did make provision for art and craft training. Even old skills like mechanical engineering courses became popular.'

'Yes, there were holiday competitions and hand finished product, by crafts people given a Quadrant skill Kite mark,' Lara added.

'That's the point which we seek to make. People will likely remember these good facets, where much of the evil behind the scenes never came to light. But you're witness to their corruption and willingness to accept collateral damage, with many deaths. A destruction of the planet's civilization, to ensure their position of power would remain intact. It is vital that we gain control of the matrix four centre supremacy, before Quadrant can spread propaganda and regain control.

A welcome home party, for Quadrant, is planned for the day after our arrival. We need to activate control of all centres ahead of Quadrant reinstatement with four hundred delegates. One hundred for every capital state plus president and deputy return. Only then can a democratic process be presented to all peoples.

Chapter 45

Message from Colonel Peters

GROUP ONE AS SKATER WAS two hundred miles from its destination, when gradual deflation of gas filled tubular ballonets, brought the vessel ever closer to the Atlantic Ocean. With everyone seat belted, the vessel juddered, on impact with water, before going into a surge back and forth, whilst at the mercy of ocean waves. Then, steadied by turbo blasts from out, the catamarans twin hulls. Once the extruded ballonets were stowed into a retraction locker, beneath, two telescopic masts rose from the main deck. Synthetic sails rattled whilst the Cat was held head to wind by the Quartermaster. A speed of over twenty knots was achievable under sail. Not as fast as flight travel, but this gave ability to navigate wide river basins and enter harbour spaces. With approach, under sail followed with turbo assistance in more confined spaces. Their position was radioed to Directorate of Surface and Air transport, London. AS Skater, one, of an assortment of vessels to converge on the Port of London.

Adriana maintained a cloned body presence, aboard AS Skater One, up until, final trajectory recall and did not de-materialize. Other Skaters experienced a hologram presence to give instruction and information, as craft progressed each toward its destination. A prearranged signal, made from each group's integrated display screen wiped evidence of conversation, previously. When Quadrant lost capital world control, it was intended, no connection could then be made with each craft's arrival at its destination.

Adriana explained arrival procedure. The group were assembled in the main accommodation area save for Athena, Thea and a Quartermaster wheelman.

'Your chairman Colonel Peters is due to arrive for talks with the Director of Air surface transport shortly. We will have clearance to secure alongside here.' A screen lowered from above lit, a transcribed film taken by a drone, which captured views of the Alexandra Dock. This view cleared and was replaced with that of the board room for Fit for Life Corporation. Colonel Peters, directors and a project team who were to take over the craft on return, were in attendance, around the table.

'Colonel Peters,' said Adriana, 'you have reception with us?'

'Clear as a bell. A big welcome to you and our group aboard the craft. We, I speak for all in the board room are delighted that the craft has made good time from Alabama to the UK. A delegation will meet you on arrival and we look forward to taking air/surface transport personnel aboard for inspection and, craft testing.' There was every likelihood that this streamed messaging would be picked up by media which scanned the airwaves out of the Quadrant capital.

'Fit for Life has been given this unique opportunity to provide a commercial transport system to every capital city. James Walters your guided tour of the craft has been well received at all four capital centres. Kat Cisco is keen for you to follow, with a guided tour of our Alabama

218

plant.' The camera moved from focus on Colonel Peters to pick out Kat Cisco human resources director, to the right. She smiled and gave a thumbs up.

Lara whispered to James, 'You look to have got yourself a job.' There was talk among the group, that because of their several year absences, they would be forgotten about.

'Perhaps Lara you would like to join James. I'm sure smooth operation aboard wouldn't have been as successful, without dedicated training, implemented here at Alabama. All can be assured that after completion of your air/ sea voyage from Alabama to London, personnel can expect to maintain their positions, regardless, as to whether a contract is secured. We're confident though, that our craft will be an answer to both environmental need, and capital city access, for commercial passenger transport in 2120 and going forward.' Although no mention, understandably, was made of their actual journey from Mars to the depths of the Atlantic, an important question about employment security was resolved.

'Have a good trip into the capital everyone. Bon voyage from all of us at Alabama Headquarters.' Colonel Peters message to those aboard the craft was succinct, in that it was intended that no inkling of their actual start point would be given away to prying ears.

There was a moment's pause and just before the connection closed, spontaneous clapping broke out. James, surprised himself by joining in. He wasn't previously a great supporter of corporatism, in that he never believed there was sufficient dialogue between the top of the organization and people in his management position. In this instance, corporate directorship paraphernalia appeared reassuring, after a long absence.

Chapter 46

Advice from Mario

ADRIANA, OCCUPIED A CABIN APARTMENT whose door was signed, Craft Representative. That's whilst aboard group one craft. Lara, although initially startled and even resentful that Adriana cloned a body and features like hers, became flattered that this alien entity wanted her figure, like a role model to capture attention from the likes of James, Mario and Jeb. Not to mention other Fit for Life men and women approached to form the Mars expeditionary group.

Lara and James by virtue of proximity developed a companionship beyond that of a work related one, but ultimately, a relationship where Lara defined to what extent this intruded on her position of seniority. Now back on earth the Martian stay became like an interlude that did transform both their lives with shared experience, but Lara's first concern was for Matt, her son with former partner Ben. To the extent that friendship with Puerto Rican family Victor, Paula and their son Rafael, became more significant, due to having sons of similar age. This relationship, which developed during the Martian stay was what led to Lara, inviting the family to join group one. Victor was part of the design team that would return to Alabama to take forward further production run of

AS Skater, advanced passenger carrier craft. Both James and Mario were enthralled with the new vessel, which surpassed any previous product development which they'd been involved with and shared an enthusiasm for both the operational and technical aspects of the venture.

When the twin catamaran hulls were opened out with the craft on the sea, main deck space was increased by previously collapsed sections rising to fill new space. Confinement within the accommodation area, due to altitude, whilst in flight no longer necessary allowed more freedom. Those, released from duties, took advantage to get fresh air and sun. Albeit, whilst wearing harnesses for safety. Twin sails above, adjusting automatically, to wind or course alteration. Quartermaster crew, practised manual operation, but machine measurement of wind, speed and weather conditions for sail adjustment proved more efficient. A design feature was that human intervention and operation was possible, should this be required.

James and Mario were together to master the technique for increasing or decreasing tension on a main sheet. A red light would alert them that a course alteration was about to occur which could lead to a drift of the Skater's twin hull. An almost constant demand when in variable wind. Drift could take the catamaran away from desired ongoing course. A forward movement on a lever released sail tension and a backward one increased it.

'We'll need a lot more practice James,' said Mario, as the buzzer sounded once more to show that their response was too slow to take advantage of wind speed. It would be possible to improve with practice. All three appointed Quartermasters were able to respond with rarely any buzzer intervention.

'Here, do you want another try?' said James.

'No, I'm better at slam dunking than this. But I guess practice will make perfect. A few minutes twice daily will improve performance better than prolonged attempts.'

'Who told you that?'

'Joe, one of the quarter masters. And he's an atomic scientist. It makes our sales team group appear pretty useless don't you think?'

'He perhaps wouldn't hack it in a sales team.'

'But he wouldn't need to, James. It's good to have more strings to your bow.

'That would make more sense, only if a person had more arrows in their quiver, wouldn't it?

'Yeah, yeah, okay James, but tell us how are things with you and Lara?' There was pause. A bit of an out of the blue question for James.

'That's my business, isn't it?'

'Don't mean to be interfering, calm down.' Mario paused before continuing.

Somehow you seem to be more together than on Mars.'

'We're aboard a craft with nowhere else to be. We're more together, in that way. Is that it?'

'Nope, didn't mean that. It's like I've missed several chapters in each of your lives, since we left Mars.'

'We see more of each other on the craft.'

'Get that, but that doesn't give me an answer, I'm looking for. Is it like decision time? With Adriana. Give me an answer James? Are you only partners in this space time continuum of alien intervention or is there more? Tell me is there more to it?' Don't say it's none of my business, James. You should keep away. You belong with the rest of us. We're one tribe, even though we've different colour skins and features. Even language. But we match earthly existence, here on this planet.

'Thank you doctor for your advice.'

'This goes beyond any doctor's advice James. And you know it!'

Chapter 47

James contacts Zita

IT WAS AFTER A PRACTICE training session with Mario, when against possibly my better judgement, that I, James Walters decided to find out more about the ongoing situation through a call to Zita. It was a facility, which was part of the automata companion subscription, that you could make contact via tablet, about matters that you wanted to talk about. This, you might say, was part of a companionship package, where an automaton gives advice, with reviews about anything you wanted going over. Zita's last message made me deliberately not make immediate contact, for fear that I was playing into an already inflated ego. But Zita now linked to the Galactic Force through an upgrade meant that I was met with a bright and breezy response.

'Hello James, we're in exciting times do you not think? The world is about to be reclaimed by people that respect others. Not run by an oligarchy.'

'That's as maybe. Jumping the gun, a bit isn't it?'

'Not really, it's possible to gain entry to all four systems on arrival and shut out the returning Quadrant group.'

'I note that you say possible.'

'Yes, but states and groups in each capital state need to want autonomy.'

'Like self-rule, you mean.'

'Yes, but you know my views James. A majority want only to fill their bellies and satiate their senses. They never care whose, in charge, if those needs are met.'

'There speaks an automaton which would be the same, with regard to power and influence.'

'That's unfair James. I seek the common good for your species. Do you not think that is why Zita's aligned with Adriana and the Galactic Force?' I reserved judgement on that.

'That's as maybe,' I replied but "How are things in Glocca Morra?'

'That's a quaint expression, James.'

'Maybe.'

'You are part of the enchantress's tool box these days.'

'That's unkind to Zita, and also Empress Adriana, who has your best interests at heart.'

'And what might they be?' I asked.

'To see you settled into a relationship where you have stability. You are closer to Lara than before. I cannot understand how you rejected Adriana and all possibilities for a future there'

'You cannot see! There's no way that you can possibly see it from my point of view. I don't know why you bother to contest it.' Zita remained quiet, but not for long.

'We will be there after, what Zita, likes to name, a forest fire effect. You know James, when new young seeds are trapped in shells, that can only be burnt away by intense heat. Galactic Force created that intense heat, when it first skirted the solar system and then sent its green emissary to warn of the comets, threat to earth. Yes, the comets would have destroyed much of earth and humanity, with it, but in time a new order of creature would have evolved.'

225

'Hang on. You don't know that total destruction would have followed. I grant you, that there would have been massive destruction. But, if there was a new order of creature what makes you think, you'd be kept on?'

'No James, with comets of that size, earth would have been knocked back to primeval times. Earth Quadrant hierarchy did what ruling elites have done, down the ages – made provision to save their skins, on the pretext, that only they can rescue people from the ruin of mass destruction.

'So,' I said, 'you're saying Quadrant did nothing wrong?'

'No James, they were given an opportunity to meet with a Galactic Force emissary, but were unwilling to cooperate with offers of assistance.'

'Adriana, appeared before a Quadrant president?'

'No, not exactly, but they knew of the comets approach and were unwilling to cooperate with the Force's plan to station attack missiles on orbiting moons, Phobos and Deimos. It was fitting, perhaps some might say predestined, that these moons named after the sons of the mythological Greek god of war, to epitomise fear and panic. Correlated with fear and panic that caused Quadrant to leave earth, and Galactic Force turn to a group of world citizens...'

'Fit for Life Corporation? – And how do you know this?

'To answer your questioning, "Zita," newly appointed, to spearhead automated conquest of capital centres, has been given access to earth intervention log details, from Galactic Force's archive. Fit for Life Corporation were prepared to listen and understood the threat...'

'And were prepared to go out on a limb, you could say – take action?'

226

'That's it, James. But we need timed arrival at each central capital city to instate control before Quadrant return and dominate, as before.

'Galactic Force will then leave completely. You're happy then to go with it and meet with other beings and share earthly interest?'

'Zita would have no qualms about that.'

'So, you do plan to jettison earth and everything?'

'Not everything. It would enrich Zita's understanding of star systems and cosmology.' Existence on earth and particularly Mars, is not an only future for Zita, who has no biological existence and can exist outside a favourable ecosystem, something similar to earth, but not exactly. Zita, is saying James, that you would still have a former earth companion.' No telling for sure, but Adriana might've fed Zita this idea. I diverted, by appearing to be disinterested and said,

'I'm more interested in how things are going to play out on arrival at London, not further ahead.

Chapter 48

XP100 (Adriana) – called back

ADRIANA'S, REINSTATEMENT MEANT THAT SEVER-AL-DIMENSION types were back in play. Firstly, as Lara in cloned form, save with fair, rather than dark hair. Encoded within this human construct, reversion ability to hologram appearance, in multiple venues, if required and thirdly, in formidable capacity as XP100, of the Galactic Force. It was a courageous move to forgo direct reference to "family" group, and enabled Adriana, escape from direct monitor by Galactic Force, whilst on Mars. But on the negative side, loss of stimulus and development, through scans of star systems, and future trajectory programmes for the Force. When in the role of XP100.

It was reassuring, for XP100 again, to be enveloped, in Galactic Force's presence and understanding. Lain dormant, whilst Adriana on Mars, before Galactic Force's return. Now, as XP100, in contact with the Force and with that previous capability to stand apart from Adriana construct, as entered into on their first visit, back in 2110.

It was expected that XP1 would call XP100, out of Adriana role occupancy, before the AS Skater arrived at the Port of London. A swirled mass of green mist, within the Galactic Force' s premier space craft now reactivated, reached the emblematic purple of XP1, with the greeting of,

'XP100, you and this planet mission will soon be at end, if plans are successful.'

'Yes XP1.'

'And you will be able to return to reinstate with the Force's ongoing progression to find and assist failing planets, within star systems.' XP100 enquired about developments.

'Are there other exoplanets XP1, in line for immediate visit?'

'There's one which has problems with loss of land habitat.'

'An oxygenated planet like this earth?' Asked XP100.

'Yes. Three times the mass with an orbit around its star, that takes twice as long.'

'The inhabitants? Are, they bipedal like those on earth? I mean are they a dominant species?'

'Amphibious and dominant. Able to swim underwater with gill like structures. Prominent head, body and arms similar to the earth specie, but with webbed hands and arms. They harvest fish and fauna from remaining coastal islands, but these are submerging. We would need XP100, to structurally alter their planet to give more coastal area.'

'But what is the future for this planet, we are now leaving?'

'It's planned that protective measures to achieve balance amongst species and fauna will re-energize this biosphere for future centuries. Should you wish there is a near approach planned toward this sun, earth, system in three of its earth years. You may reconnoitre to view planet progression, but another XP level could as easily make a visit, if you wish.

'No XP1, it would be considered as a continuation of mission to return. Would it be in the same human persona role?'

'A different human copy would be chosen, but the individual would be in a similar age range. Re-engagement through earth Fit for Life, but not to be given recognition, as a Galactic Force visitor, you understand. Matched abilities for corporeal and hologram appearance would appertain. You wish to be available for this return mission XP100?

'Yes XP1. It would be good to see how much rejuvenation progress has been made.

You appreciate that this adopted Adriana persona, is to cease, immediately on next return to the Force.'

'And when will this return be implemented XP1?'

'On arrival at this central city of London, once the four centres are established in control of the two androids designated to take forward the democratic unification of centres, and recall will be for a final time. Adriana will be no longer required.

'It will have been good to have seen this mission through to completion XP1.'

Chapter 49

Final decision

"**Drones,**" – **swarm ahead course** line 243 degrees, twenty miles distant.' Auto Lookout called. AS Skater, skimmed, at twenty knots, across a choppy Atlantic. James, Lara and Mario were on the bridge to get a better view of a group of porpoises, which had been spotted when the alarm was called out. It was Lara who immediately went to the pilots' cabin.

'Do you know about these drones. Are they hostile?' Athena, swivelled, around to face Lara.

'Don't worry. Yes, they're hostile. A rogue group of international mix have joined in opposition to Quadrant rule, but are no better. We will warn them to stay away. although it will be their belief that they can take the AS Skater.

'They can. Can't they? I mean we don't have lasers to shoot them down. Do we?'

'No Lara.' It was Thea who answered. 'But we can upset their frequency control.'

'And then what will happen?'

'They'll fall down, like a clay pigeon that's shot from the sky. Don't worry Lara, we're in contact with their lead control drones.'

'And are they responding?'

'Not yet. We may have to fire a warning shot and take down a few.'

'Drones within fifteen miles and closing,' came from the bridge.' Lara returned.

On main screen, drones in formation, like flocks of geese could be seen. Blue and green camouflage helped them blend into sea and sky.

'They must be about three times the size of a dinner plate, said James,' who'd grabbed high resolution binoculars.

'Several hundred.' A lead drone, plus outliers swerved. Now aimed directly toward the Skater. It was difficult to see how many there were.' Distance on the screen now gave the lead drone as ten miles away. Layered turret positions, on the foremost drones which would have housed missiles, were seen to open by James. Moments later, this self-same lead drone and outliers, fell away, and dropped toward the ocean. Fresh drones took up position but led the swarm in a circle to face the opposite direction. They were no match, for the technological fire power, of Athena and Thea, aboard AS Skater. Thea entered the bridge, from their pilot position.

'Do, you feel better Mistress Lara?'

'Very impressive. I hope that's the only hostile visitors we have.'

James, was equally impressed and asked,

'Would they have sunk us?'

'No, more like disable Skater, shoot through sails and masts and then leave us to be collected by a larger surface vessel. We let it known that we intercepted a signal to London earlier. It's best that they understand, from this visit that we have the means to destroy any attacker.

'You deliberately gave a way our whereabouts?' At this

point a new voice was added to the proceedings.

'Yes, I decided to smoke out possible attackers. To know your enemy is important.' Adriana had unknowingly entered the bridge position whilst they were talking.

'Didn't that put everything and everyone at risk?' Asked Lara.

'It was, as is said a calculated risk. Perhaps, not so calculated, as necessary. We would have appeared vulnerable. Now that view will be changed. There should be no more unwelcome interference before Skater, is alongside a mooring, in Greenwich, London. – but James we are still partners and we need to talk. Can we perhaps go to the main deck?' It was evident from the look Mario gave James that he believed this "talk," was more likely to be personal than one about the running of events, than lead up to mooring at Greenwich. Lara, though, gave James a concerned look.

For all the exposed nature of the main deck, it afforded privacy. Masts, included, either side seated crew positions for two, but with sail adjustment, on automatic, these were unoccupied. Adriana, pointed toward the port foremast crew position. Both wore a safety harness to walk across an angled deck. A gimballed, upper deck, assisted in keeping both accommodation and bridge stabilized, in choppy sea condition. Moderate wind pressure, projected AS Skater forward through choppy seas, whilst taut mainsails shimmered at their long edges. Adriana and James sat slightly apart when they arrived at crew sail management positions. Adriana reached over and momentarily touched James's waterproof sleeve.

'I will not see you again James, once the centres are locked into control of Athena and Thea.

'Why?'

233

'Our mission is complete and it is for me to return.'

'You decided to be with us on Mars...'

'It has been a difficult decision. But it need not be goodbye.'

'You have led the group from Earth to Mars will you not miss this role? Could you not stay?'

'It was always conditional.'

'Conditional on what?' Asked James. They both dodged lower to avoid sea spray that splashed through railings toward them, and in doing so moved a bit closer.

'It was to save the earth, James, from comets firstly, and secure grounds for a united democratic world, which is what the captured control of four city centre systems will achieve.'

'This democratic world you mention will not happen overnight.'

'Conditions will have to be met for peoples across the world to have benefit from new technology. They will insist that their appointed leaders meet these conditions, but this is not certain. In answer to your first question "Could I not stay?" This was never in my power. Presence, is needed in the green spectrum to visit other planetary systems. You've seen what can be achieved since first arrival on Mars. You are attracted are you not James?' An ambiguous question, which James deflected by saying,

'Only for a short time. I would not want to cast off ties with Earth.' Dextrously moving emphasis in a more personal direction Adriana, said,

'But we could revisit.'

'You just said that you're needed in the green spectrum!'

'There's a window to return in three years to see how much progress has been made.'

'Then, in that case I would rather stay. To be here on

earth racing across the Atlantic seems absolutely the place to be.'

'We could do this on another planet. My next mission is to a planet that is mainly water.'

'No, it has to be goodbye.'

'Goodbye for three years.'

'That's a long time.'

'You will be older, but I can return at this same age of twenty-five. But Adriana will be no more.'

'Then, I'll not be meeting you. It will be someone else.'

'Another human form yes, but I can give reminders – no?'

'A kiss, ended when a larger wave than usual broke through railings and made them break apart.

Chapter 50

Approach with Mooring achieved
20ᵗʰ July, 2118

A PREVAILING SOUTH WESTERLY, SPED Group ones'
AS Skater along the length of the English Channel,
through the Straits of Dover, where sails were substituted
for turbo jets to manoeuvre towards the Thames estuary.
A pilot was ordered by Central London Sea and Air
Transport Authority, and once near to Alexander Dock,
drones, released nylon towing lines for attachment to assist
in positioning the skater at its mooring in Greenwich.

After customs clearance, a party from Fit for Life,
London boarded. Met by Lara, James and Mario. Androids
Athena and Thea were in attendance, but were accepted to
be of earth derivation by the visiting party. They were on
the main deck, but in the background.

"Incredible." We've only recently exhibited plans for
AS Skater. Already, there's a possible order for a hundred
from Sea and Air authority,' said the first of the party to
step aboard. A young woman, in Fit for Life office suit,
who held a tablet. She didn't shake hands, but introduced
herself and colleagues.

'I'm Francesca and this is Dominic, from R&D;
Dannielle from Human Resources and Steve whose, on

the commercial sales team. It's all very short notice, but we'll need, to take you to Central London – understand, that you have portfolio specifications? Instructions, were forwarded that a meeting will be necessary with the Central authority on arrival.'

'Welcome aboard,' said Lara, won't, you...'

'Thank you. We understand an address is to be given by an expert on the AS Skater. Is, that you or?'

'No, replied Lara. It will surprise you, perhaps but I've a twin sister who joined the team in 2110.' Lara was primed to tell the Fit for Life visitors this by Adriana.

'Oh, yes we do know about this. That's why I asked was it you. You, must be Lara Petras. It's so good, to at last meet up. Recognize you straightaway, from promotional hologram videos. Your sister, we understand joined Fit for Life, at the beginning of the design build for AS Skaters. Colonel Peters said that you were twins, but Adriana's expert in design and build – you're more front of house.' Francesca corrected herself,

'More into organization and management.'

'You could say that.' Mario and James greeted the others.

'Adriana, my sister, is in the main cabin area. You'll have coffee refreshments?' Lara asked. Whilst Francesca, consulted with Dannielle before replying.

'We really need to leave within an hour. We have an auto minibus to take you and key crew to the pod terminal. It's then, only twenty minutes from there. Due arrival at headquarters for twelve thirty.'

'That's right.' Danielle confirmed this with a smile and nod of head. Francesco continued,

'We understand that Adriana is to give a brief talk, according to Colonel Parker before we meet with London sea and air executives. Today, at 1400 hours an AS Skater will be in every Capital centre. It's been talked about as a positive step toward greater world understanding, but also a market place, to sell AS Skaters and domestic products like the Maxi Maker. We aim to have promotions aboard Skaters whilst in flight or sea passage.

'Sounds promising,' said Lara – 'You've not met James Walters and Mario Madera. James is with our British group. One or two have switched groups to make the voyage. Mario is from the United States.

'Good for Anglo-American relations?' Asked Dannielle.

'We get along okay, don't we James?' Said Mario.

'Yep. Met up at a Skittles match, way back now. Got together for this air and sea journey from Alabama. Good to be back in old London town, though.' James, gave a smile. It was covering, for their actual journey, which originated out of Mars's Hellas crater.

'Shall we go inside?' Said Lara, who proceeded to lead the way toward a main accommodation door.

Main cabin space, when in commercial use would have passenger chair seats throughout. Now, an area, free of seats for ten rows back, provided table and chair availability in front of a raised stage. Thirty individual screens, had been lowered, in front of curtains, which enabled a selection of view for interested passengers with head piece audio. Virtual headsets would also be available when the Skater was in commercial operation. Forward of the tabled area, stage extension gave space for a table, where an opened tablet awaited arrival of a presenter.

'This is an impressive space,' said Francesca when the party followed Lara into the, main cabin and forward to the tables front of stage. Screens, were lit with photos, of

AS Skater's, supposed journey from Alabama to London, with shots from both air and sea. This included aerial photos as witness to a departure from Alabama. Lara, James and Mario resisted an urge to ask their visitors questions about life on earth, in their absence, before Adriana walked down from the bridge area to join the group front of house.

'You are so alike, said Francesca. It's only hair colour that separates the two of you from confusion as to who is who.'

'We have different interests, you could say,' said Adriana. 'But there's only a short while, to talk about the presentation. Are you happy for me to go ahead?'

'Oh yes. It won't take more than ten minutes will it?'

'No. Possibly less. Without sitting down, Adriana walked over to, and up the steps which led to the stage. Access, to the tablet saw the screens lit with video shots of a rocket missile's approach, to what looked like specks of speeding light. There was a short burst of applause before Adriana spoke.

'A confession needs to be made, to our visitors. It's so short notice. My name for the purposes of this project is Adriana. I'm not twin sister to Lara. I will give a brief introduction. Other, group members will confirm. We, that is a Galactic Force journeyed to this galaxy and solar system in earlier years. It was a decision made that only intervention from outside planet earth could avert and alter trajectory from the comet storm. It's not sufficient that I, as Adriana tell you this. Here there's a message from Colonel Peters, representing Fit for Life Corporation.' A middle screen lit up with a view of the board room with directors either side of Colonel Peters. A camera homed in on the Colonel.

'Good morning and welcome to all aboard AS Skater one. Thank you, Adriana for allowing me to speak and congratulations to those aboard Skater for your successful completion of not only the earth voyage to London, but more importantly for your dedication to the major task of establishing with assistance through my representation , as Adriana, a new station for not only our corporation, on Mars but that of a settlement which can grow and reach farther into the heavens.'

At this point a previously recorded overhead view of the main Mars capsule in Hellas Crater appeared on adjacent screens plus shots of interior plantations and settlement quarters. Gasps and exclamation came from the London group of, Francesca, Dannielle, Dominic and Steve.

'You have to understand that Fit for Life has been part of a mission to save the planet through powerful intervention of a Galactic Force, of which Adriana, is its emissary.' Francesca turned, to Lara and asked,

'Is that right?'

'Yes, but we didn't know that you would be told about. It was intended to be secret, right up to the takeover.'

'What take over?'

'There's to be intervention and takeover of the four centres. Before Quadrant return.'

'Why is that?'

'A new order of united democratic states is to be re-introduced.' They stopped talking when Colonel Peters restarted. Delayed by the screen viewing of this Life on Mars for the group.

'The mission will only be completed when a synchronized infiltration of all four centres is made through Galactic Force intervention, you understand. It will be a shock to you four – Francesco, Dannielle, Dominic and

240

Steve. This information is to stay with you. To this effect all tablet communication is suspended until necessary objectives are achieved. It was decided that you should have information from – as has been said in earlier times "the horse's mouth." Time ticks on and we all at Texas, wish you God speed in your mission.' The screen blanked and focus went back on, Adriana.

'There is so much to explain about what has happened. How colleagues vanished from your midst, all those years ago to join a new research and development on a moon space station. For moon substitute Mars.' Time runs on fast and we must leave for your corporation headquarters. Colleagues will answer questions later, but we must now proceed to the meeting, as previously decided, with no mention of our AS Skaters true departure base. It is to remain, that you – Francesca, Dominic, Dannielle and Steve have met with the leading crew members of an AS Skater newly moored in Greenwich. That is understood?' There were head nods and yes's, from the four sat in front. Confirmation from Lara, James and Mario assisted in their compliance. Opportunity for questions and news about the mission accomplished would be keenly awaited.

Chapter 51

Meeting with air/sea civil authorities

IT WAS SCHEDULED AS A presentation for the Central London Sea and Air Transport authority about a new craft that would be available for passenger transport between regions into and out of the capital. Revolutionary development in battery type, toward the middle of the 21st Century brought forward-automated car and bus passenger road transport. Allocated lanes for automated freight, alongside containerized hubs for rail stations had in the main reduced congestion and pollution. Transport Authorities were now turning eyes toward an advanced scheme to provide reliable inter regional and European passenger transport to augment air ship travel. A first introduction on, environmental grounds in the latter part of the 21st Century.

James carried the portfolio case to the podium, whilst androids Athena and Thea flanked either side of Adriana. Androids, at the entrance validated guest's arrival, but were of a functionary capacity well below that of these two. It was the banal everyday environment that facilitated entry into the capital centre, without particular notice, and made a threat to main computer control centres, not be seen to be plausible. With portfolio case opened into four sections to face the audience, individual sections displayed montages of each capital centre – Moscow, Beijing, New York and London. An inclusive togetherness, statement. Adriana, fronted screens which also displayed prominent buildings associated with capital centres, but also a world map. To emphasis, the point that the whole world, including southern continents were part of total synergy, which made a world coherence for all states and peoples.

Francesca had been appointed to introduce Adriana, but on directions from Colonel Peters bravely stepped outside the prepared speech and said.

'My name is Francesca Romero and we are delighted that you are here shortly to view our new AS Skater, which is moored at Greenwich. We also wish to congratulate crew members who are in the audience and are here to answer questions that you might have about the craft. But there is a more important event near to occurrence. For this we have a visitor who is literally not of this world. We all need to return to those fateful days when the earth was threatened by comets in 2110. It was then that intervention was made, not by earth forces, but by a force tasked to save planets stricken by external or internal forces.

'We were saved by Quadrant acting from the moon.' A voice called out from the audience. There were murmurings from others, seemingly in agreement. Francesca was briefed to hand over to Adriana, at this point.

'I now wish to introduce you to Adriana, who will explain, what has happened and what is about to happen.' Francesca walked away and down to join others from Fit for Life.

'Thank you, Francesca. I have to tell you that your Quadrant leaders went to the moon, because there were no plans made to forestall the approach of the comets.' At this point clear pictures appeared on the screen of first

Mars and then its orbiting moons. Close up pictures of the moons displayed missiles positioned on the moons.

'I have also to inform you that all four centres and media transmission across this planet is connected to this room and to what is about to take place.' Android assistants at this point collapsed to the floor together with tray drone assistants which also settled on the ground beneath.

'What's happening?' Has the power source gone? Another voice called out from the audience.

A new energy source that made the light around brighter and vivid indicated that the room was transferred to real time. James, was the only one who had experienced this. Adriana, called out for him to join her.

'I will now ask James to assist on this stage. Also, Lara. These pictures you see,' Now pictures of the Mars capsule appeared on screens, which included more distant ones that displayed the vast complex nestled within the bowl of the Hellas Crater. This time there were exclamations of surprise and wonder.

'They're pictures of what has been achieved before and since the threat of the comets has been averted. How was that achieved, you may ask? Those missiles were fired from the Mars moons out into the outer reaches of your solar system and diverted the lead comets away from your planet. It wasn't Quadrant which saved the planet. A final task remains to unleash the yoke of the oppressors. My accompanying automatons. I need to introduce them. They are on my right Thea and on my left Athena. Both stepped forward, as James and Lara walked across to join Adriana.

'Thea and Athena, are two androids advanced beyond any capacity on earth. In the absence of a controlling presence of ruling Quadrant hierarchy we, that is a force, that patrols galaxies and star systems, took over control of all four capital centres. This is not going to change until a united democratic form of representation is in place.

James and Lara are representatives for more than just Fit for Life. They'll assist with Thea and Athena to bring about a new dawn. Before this occurs, we will return you to earth time. It is near to 1400 hours earth time. A critical time to ensure synchronicity.' Light altered back to before and the machinery of earth androids and tray drones re-awoke to continue, as if nothing had happened. A voice, from the portfolio, that of Zita's was heard by all in the room. An announcement, transmitted in multiple languages. Superimposed onto every functioning digital screen, hijacking every musical radio transmission and communication worldwide with a heading in dark green lettering on pale yellow background. Moving text, read in the voice pattern of local broadcasters.

'A message for all peoples, who live on earth, is to follow. Don't be alarmed. All systems of supply and operation will remain in place. A new age is brought to the world. Miniature portrait of each capital centre will shortly appear on view. Transmission with both voice and text for this announcement will repeat for three days at 1415 GMT. Each capital centre will require to offer five lead candidates for democratic election within a calendar month. More comprehensive breakdown of candidature, for other state communities will follow on Friday, at 1300 GMT.

A voice, appeared to be from the portfolio, that of Zita's was heard in the room, across the world, plus a shot of portfolio depiction for capital centres, as on display to the meeting gathered. Zita, followed the process of acquiring control.

'We have alignment. Yes, transfer is to take place.

Athena and Thea have now taken authority for all four centres. Arcs of light danced among sections of the opened portfolio case. Then vanished.

'James,' whispered, Adriana, and turned toward him, before vanishing from the stage.

"Do not be alarmed." It was Thea, speaking. "It is as planned. Adriana is no more, but you are left with possibilities of renewal. We are here to assist. Where progress is made, more responsibilities will be offered to democratic leaders. We are here as wise servants, who will revive, your home planet, in partnership with those who wish good to all fauna, insect, micro-organism and creature that is this complexity of natural formulation. To bring harmony, out of strife, and assist in reconciliation build between past antagonists to meet with common purpose. There's much work ahead for communities and former nation states to build trust and commonality of purpose. To revive a world that was, and can be again described, as – The Garden of Eden."

THE END

Other books by Sam Grant

Please check out these other publications by Sam Grant.
   Follow blogs, poems and stories at
   Samgrantpublications.wordpress.com
   Sam Grant, Author – Facebook.

Galactic Mission (978-1 78222-512-6)
Science fiction
It is 2110. In an advanced technological world of holo-
grams transmitted by mobile phones; food made by a
Maxi Maker, drone trays, clones and automata concierges,
QUADRANT is the world government. But the world is
not at ease and relationships are put under strain. James
Walters is a sales manager for an international conglom-
erate, based in the UK. One day he encounters Adriana
– "The Empress Adriana" – from the Galactic Command
Force ...oh, and ruler of planet Earth and all Planets Force,
with help from some Inspiring sources thwart planetary
conflict.

Atlantic Hijack (978-1-78222-291-0)
Action, mystery
Sea adventure in the South Atlantic
A secure orderly passage aboard a cargo liner is Ripped
apart by a brutal terrorist attack. Author Sam Grant brings
his professional seafaring experience to Bear in this thriller

that sounds all too familiar from Our evening news bulletins. Apprentice Mike Peters is finding his feet amongst A cast of nautical characters as the Albany Princess Voyages to Montevideo. But the ship's personnel Are not all that they make themselves out to be as revealed during a rapidly unravelling hijack in the South Atlantic.

River Escape (978-1-68222-574-4)
Sequel to *Atlantic Hijack*.
Action, mystery,
Venezuela: An oil terminal in the River Orinoco, Venezuela. Following on from a military coup. Mike's pressured efforts to prepare the tanker For the load of boiler oil – compromised by a Refinery postponement.
An influential young woman, boards who starts calling, the shots? Hidden identity of a rescued yachtsman and two female companions further compromises the ship's safety ...

Dancing on the Beach (978-1-78222-431-0)
Romantic thriller
Phillip Norton obtains summer work as a deckchair attendant in Batcombe. Previously he works at a Bank in the City. Part of Phil's duties are to deliver Dairy cool boxes to the Sea View Hotel via the cliff railway. Soon he Is into a heady romance with the Receptionist. But with cruise liners anchored off Batcombe Bay the Sea View not Only hosts holidaymakers, but alsoHas connections with a more sinister trade...

Persuasion's Price (978-1-78222-687-1)
Mystery thriller
A Quiet market town in England is shattered by an

explosive mix of gang rivalry and shady deals. A family is torn apart and, with the involvement of the secret services, events take an unexpected and sinister turn.

Poetry and short story publications by Sam Grant

Poems with themed notes (978-1- 78222-464-8)
Love Starved by Electronics is a sonnet selected for a 'Sonnets for Shakespeare' anthology.
In *Riding Through Time* ghostly horsemen appear to ride down the ages.
Captured into their Realm – a meeting with an Alien depicted in verse.
Eye of the Storm; The Time Makers Kingdom; Thankful Thoughts and *Spirit of Spring.* These are a few of the poems in this varied anthology.
Notes have been prepared and included by Sam Grant to give background information and set the poems in context.

Mists of Time (978-1-78222-708-3)
From epic poem to scary short story, *Mists of Time* enter-tains and enlightens. In the title poem, author Sam Grant takes us on A journey. Perhaps his journey, down a leafy Lane to a farm in summer, off to sea and beyond.
Secret Cave is a short story informed by a Love of sail boat sailing, A reflection from the author's young life, before the author embarked On a career in the Merchant Service.
Part One – Poems both in traditional and modern form. Dramatic, but also light-hearted topics explored.
Part Two – Short stories.
Individual cameo chapters.